savage gods

SAVAGE HEARTS BOOK TWO

AMANDA RICHARDSON

Savage Gods
Amanda Richardson
Published by Amanda Richardson
© Copyright 2022 Amanda Richardson
www.authoramandarichardson.com

Editing by Nice Girl, Naughty Edits
Cover Design by Moonstruck Cover Design & Photography
Photographer: Wander Aguiar

This is a work of fiction. Names, characters, businesses, places, events and incidents are either the products of the author's imagination or used in a fictitious manner. Any resemblance to actual persons, living or dead, or actual events is purely coincidental.

All rights reserved. This book or any portion thereof may not be reproduced or used in any manner whatsoever without the express written permission of the author except for the use of brief quotations in a book review.

author's note

Savage Gods is an enemies-to-lovers reverse harem romance. It is a spin-off of the Ruthless Royals duet, and takes place in the same world (with some crossover in later books).

Please note that this is book two in the Savage Hearts series. While it does not end with a true cliffhanger, there are unanswered questions still to be resolved in book three, which releases on May 10, 2022. You can preorder Savage Reign here.

Please note the trigger warnings in the blurb, which is located on the next page.

As always, thank you for reading, and enjoy!

blurb

I would forever be grateful that Silas Huxley, Damon Brooks, and Jude Vanderbilt saved me from my own broken darkness.

They were there to catch me—as friends, and now as roommates and lovers. Three enigmatic, brutal gods who would do anything for me—*even kill*.

Because someone connected to Silas is planning our demise—someone with a past that doesn't want to be found.

Despite this, I know the guys will keep me safe. After all, I belong to them now.

I'm confident the four of us can withstand anything.

Until Jude disappears.

And I'll rot in hell before I let anyone hurt him.

BLURB

Welcome to the dark side of Savage Ink, motherf*ckers.

Savage Gods (Savage Hearts Book Two) is a spinoff of the Ruthless Royals duet, which does not have to be read first. It is a full-length enemies-to-lovers/bully reverse harem romance, and while it doesn't end with a true cliffhanger, there will be unanswered questions. It is advised to read the series in order. Please note Savage Gods contains explicit language, violence, guns, assault, cult-like scenarios, and kidnapping. The series will have a HEA.

For Priscilla.

Enjoy Chapter Thirteen.

one

Silas
Ten Years Ago

I run my fingers over the cut crystal, wondering how the hell anyone manages to throw a high-school party with glass cups rather than plastic solo cups. How is there not more glass on the floor? How many of these crystal tumblers does Noah Adelmann have to replace every weekend so his parents don't notice?

My mind immediately goes to the pizza boxes Ledger and I have to hide every Sunday evening before our parents get back from wherever the hell they've been preaching about the second coming. Ever since they joined the Church of the Rapture when I was six, they haven't allowed us to eat junk food.

Or celebrate holidays, or birthdays.

They believe they need healthy bodies to combat evil and healthy minds to speak to God. Sometimes I wish my parents were normal, but I know everyone in this town has secrets of their own. Greythorn is notorious for sweeping things under the rug and presenting a perfect façade of a town. None of it is real, and I can't wait to get the hell out of here next month.

I send Ledger a quick text, letting him know I'll be home soon. At fourteen, he's self-sufficient enough that I don't really have to worry about him if I leave him alone for a few hours. He's probably just lifting weights, or hanging with Hunter, one of his friends. I'm not quite sure where he'd be without them.

Without me.

I look over at Damon. His nose is stuck in his phone, and I can tell he's playing solitaire. Jude is leaning back against the soft couch, sipping the beer he brought from home. No one says anything about us being here, and truth be told, I'm not quite sure what made us choose to come tonight. We'd never been to one of these parties. Maybe it was because we'd all graduated high school earlier today. Or maybe it was because a small part of me needed tonight to let this place go.

To let these *people* go.

One, in particular.

The nerves in my body fire up as Lennon Rose makes her way through the crowd. She's wearing a short dress that shows off her legs, and I'm jealous of the way she strides into a room like she owns it. Like she gives zero fucks. Her eyes scan the room, and I know she's looking for Noah.

I hate her.

I can't stop thinking about her.

And judging by the way Damon and Jude are looking at her, they feel the same way.

"I'm going upstairs," Jude declares, scowling in Lennon's direction. She doesn't notice us. It's like her eyes never see us. Or she never *lets* herself see us. If she did, she'd have something to say about it.

"Me too," Damon says slowly, setting his crystal glass down.

I set mine next to his. "What's upstairs?" I ask, eyeing them both suspiciously.

Jude just smirks at Damon. "I want to see what Noah Adelmann keeps in his room."

We get up and I follow them upstairs. I don't exactly want to rifle through the pervert's things, and I'm starting to regret being here in his house. Not only is he notorious for dating girls way younger than him, but there are also rumors he doesn't exactly ask for consent before making a move on them. His latest conquest is none other than Lennon Rose.

Jude opens the third bedroom as we get upstairs. Of course, he knows exactly which room is Noah's. It's sparse, and I know it's because he lives on campus most of the time. Jude begins to rummage through his things, and Damon helps him. They pull apart drawers, picking through the clothes. Jude opens Noah's laptop, and I see him clicking in his emails. After he's done, he begins rearranging the things on his desk. None of it matters to me. Noah is the kind of guy who will always win in the end. A misplaced notebook isn't going to deter him if his father is there to clean up all of his messes. I'm just about to ask Jude what the point of all of this is when we hear a girl scream from the next room.

All three of us rush to the bathroom, which is adjoined to that very room. Jude slowly pushes the other bedroom door open. The room is dark, but the light from the hallway is enough to illuminate Noah Adelmann pinning Lennon Rose to the bed–and her terrified expression.

"You fucking want this," he snarls. "But I think you're too young to realize it, so how about we play a game?"

She tries to shove his hand away, but he holds it in place.

"What we have is special. No one else understands. Especially not your friends," Noah says quietly, his tone menacing. His hand moves down to her thighs. "If it would make you feel better, we can keep this a secret. Just between you and me."

White-hot anger flares through me, and I take a step forward. Lennon cries against Noah's hands, and my chest cracks in half despite the hatred I normally feel for her.

"Get your fucking hands off her." My loud voice rumbles through the room, surprising me.

Noah drops his hand just as Jude switches the light on.

"Who's there?" Noah asks, looking around in the wrong direction.

All three of us step into the bedroom. Lennon doesn't look at us. She doesn't even acknowledge what just happened. I don't expect gratitude, but I also don't expect the way her cheeks redden as she looks at Noah.

"Oh," Noah says, laughing. "Get the fuck out of here, you dorks. This party is for cool people only."

Lennon pulls her dress down and begins to walk away.

"Where the fuck do you think you're going, Lennon?" Noah asks, taking a threatening step toward her that has me moving forward too.

Lennon turns around and crosses her arms, a look of pure anger on her pretty little face.

"I'm leaving, Noah."

And then she's gone, and Jude pulls us both into the bathroom, through Noah's bedroom, and down the hallway as quickly as possible.

"Hey," he shouts at us.

I turn around. "We're leaving."

That seems to appease him, because he clenches his jaw and turns around, going back to sulk in his bedroom, presumably. *Good.* I hope his mismatched socks drive him crazy for months to come. After that, the three of us find a dark corner with a couch to sit on. We watch as Lennon and her friend Mindy begin to dance to the music. As the night wears on, we all hold out, invisible in the corner of the room. I think we all feel some sort of protectiveness toward her now, some sort of responsibility for how her night turns out. She walks to the bathroom, and Noah's eyes track her until she disappears around a corner.

I don't have to say anything to the guys. They get up and follow me, and we all keep watch of the hallway as she uses the restroom. When she exits, Damon steps forward, and she nearly collides with him.

"Sorry," Damon says.

"Watch where you're going," she snaps back at him.

Jude and I flank Damon, and her eyes go wide before they settle on me–a look of both embarrassment and loathing in her narrowed, hazel eyes.

"Lennon," I say softly, trying to convey that we understand. We get it. Maybe we're not that different, and no one–not even a monster like her–deserves to be sexually assaulted.

But she doesn't understand what I'm trying to relay, because she growls and shoves me backward so hard that I hit the wall behind me.

"Lennon," I repeat, sternly this time. "Stop."

I want to say *I understand*. I want to tell her that we can call a truce. It's graduation night, after all. Jude and Damon come to stand next to me, and her eyes flit between the three of us.

"Stop what? Get out of my way, dorks."

"Did he hurt you?" Jude asks gently.

She turns to face Jude. "I'm fine. Get out of my way."

She pushes past Damon.

I want to try one last thing. One last sentence to let her know that maybe she doesn't have to be such a monster. It doesn't have to be like this.

"I see you, Lennon."

She spins around to face me again, rage contorting her features. And then? Tears. They make her eyes glisten, bringing out the gold in the center of her irises. *God, she's beautiful even when she cries.*

"Lennon?" Noah comes around the corner, glancing between the four of us. "What's going on?"

Lennon turns to face Noah, and in an instant, I know exactly what she's about to say.

"If you ever touch me again, I will call the cops." Her words cut me straight down to my core.

Noah pushes me against the wall before I can say anything, and I grimace as he digs my spine against the stone.

"What the fuck did you do to her, you piece of shit?"

A few people come around the corner to see what's going on, and then a few of Noah's friends grab Jude and Damon. Lennon walks away.

There's no point in denying it, no point in trying to explain. It will only make us seem more guilty. The three of us look at each other for a second, and we all have the same expression on our faces.

Resignation.

We're dragged out to the front of the house, and Noah's first punch to my nose makes me cry. I wish they told you how much it fucking hurts to get punched in the face. My eyes well with tears, and a few people snicker as they watch Noah kick me in the nuts.

I collapse at the same time as Damon, and his hand brushes against mine briefly. Jude falls next, and something warm and sticky coats my upper lip. I wipe the blood away and try to stand, but Noah kicks me in the ribs, and I collapse again, my breath ragged.

Everything hurts.

So. Fucking. Much.

I hear Damon grunt as he hits the pavement again, and Jude follows shortly after, swearing as he writhes in pain. People are cheering Noah on, and just when I don't think I can pull myself up again, I do–and so do my friends. We stand, and we glare at Noah, fists clenched, shaking.

"You'll be sorry for this one day," Jude threatens. People burst out laughing all around us, and suddenly I'm even more furious.

"Oh, yeah?" Noah teases, laughing with the others. "What are you going to do?" he taunts, and when I look at Jude, he's not smiling. He's just watching Noah, and the look on his face makes me second guess how well I know my friend. The sight of his face sends shivers down my spine. Noah sees it too, because his smile drops from his face.

"I guess you'll just have to wait and see," Jude croons, smiling. The blood running down his mouth and chin makes him look completely unhinged.

I don't attempt to get up the next time Noah kicks me. Instead, I curl up in a fetal position.

I promise myself that this is the last time I let Lennon Rose fuck with my life.

two

Lennon
Present

I stop dead in my tracks outside of Savage Ink when I see Silas holding up a baby that *has* to be related to him somehow. They both have the same sandy blonde hair, the same golden skin, and the same dimples in their cheeks. The baby can't be older than six months. A man comes and sits next to him, reaching for the baby, and I smirk as I push the door open.

"You two have to be brothers, right?" I ask, sauntering up to Silas and the stranger.

Silas stands and shows me the baby, a proud look on his face. "This is my nephew, Easton." His voice is so gentle, it makes my chest ache and constrict. "And my brother, Ledger."

I look over at Ledger. What in the world do these Huxley brothers eat for breakfast? I'm just about to ask when he reaches a hand out.

"Hi," he says, looking at me, a piece of light blonde hair falling over his forehead. He's the same height as Silas, and like his brother, he's covered in tattoos. I'm sure there's a story I'm missing here. His blue eyes are a shade darker than Silas's, and he's built more like an athlete. They both have the chiseled jaws of Viking Gods.

"Nice to meet you." I smile. "I'm Lennon. I work here."

Silas cocks his head in my peripheral. "Come on. Give yourself some credit." He turns to face Ledger. "This is Lennon, and yes, she does work here, but she's also our newest roommate and..." he trails off, shrugging. "Girlfriend?"

I twist my lips to the side. "We haven't made anything official."

Ledger chuckles. "Sounds like my partner."

"Oooh, I like the term partner," I say quickly. "Girlfriend reminds me of middle school."

Silas cocks his head. "Fine. My partner."

"*Our* partner," Damon corrects from across the room, and I nearly jump. I didn't know he was even here yet.

My cheeks redden, and I look over at Ledger. We've only *just* started this... thing... between all four of us. I wasn't even sure if we were dating–but I guess it's official now? I haven't even considered how we'd introduce ourselves to the public yet. Technically, we're in a polyamorous relationship, but everything that word entails is still so new to me. I have no idea how receptive people will be, and the last thing I want is for Silas's brother to judge me before he even gets to know me.

"It's fine," he says quietly, cradling Easton in his large biceps. "My partners and I are also in a poly relationship."

My eyebrows shoot up. "Oh?"

He grins. "Must run in the family."

Before I can respond, a woman walks through the front door. She's gorgeous–short brown hair, light gray eyes, and a backpack that's nearly the same size as she is. I stifle a laugh as it gets caught in the door frame, and then I run over to help her.

"Here you go." I loop the fabric back over the handle so she can get free.

She gives me a grateful smile. "Thanks. Mom life," she jokes, pointing to Easton over my shoulder. "Hope for the best, prepare for the worst. I could feed a family of twelve from this thing for days."

We both laugh, and I hold out my hand. "I'm Lennon."

She tilts her head to the side. "Lennon? *The* Lennon?"

I narrow my eyes. "Depends on what you've heard."

She winks. "I'm Briar. Ledger's partner." She looks over my shoulder, and I see the way her eyes find Easton and Ledger–the way they soften. She turns back to me. "We should get coffee sometime," she says quickly. "I live in Greythorn now." Shaking her head, she grins. "I have a feeling we have a lot more in common than we think."

"Sure," I say, trying to process everything happening.

Silas's brother also has multiple partners, and they have a *child*. A whole new possible future opens up at this realization, settling something deep inside me.

She gives me a warm smile before brushing past me and taking Easton, hugging him like she hasn't seen him in years. I rub my neck with my hand, trying to loosen the knot surely stuck somewhere in there, and then I clear my throat when I see Silas looking in my direction.

Ledger, Briar, and Easton leave soon after that, and I busy myself with the calendar for the next hour. I ignore every knowing smile Silas sends my way, and by the time Jude saunters in, the night takes off, and clients come and go every few minutes. It's not a hard job, but it is busy. I hardly have any time to do anything between seven and one. People are constantly in because the guys book up back-to-back. I mean, Silas has appointments *two years* from now.

I hardly even know what I'll eat for dinner tonight.

By the time two o'clock rolls around, I'm exhausted and starving. The four of us pile into Jude's car as we head home.

Home.

It's still weird to say, still weird to acknowledge the fact that I now live with Silas, Damon, and Jude. It's only been four days, and these four days have been particularly busy. I've seen Mindy and Lola–neither of whom knows about my situation with the guys, or my new living arrangements. And then there's work, which takes up most of my time. My schedule is now pushed out a few hours since I'm awake until three most mornings. Late mornings and early afternoons are usually my only free time, and the guys are almost always in the home gym.

Don't get me wrong, watching the three of them work out is like watching porn. In fact, just today, I may have gotten off in the shower thinking about the way Jude's gray sweatpants hung off his hips as he lifted giant barbells. If I had any doubt about why or how they bulked out after college, it's now crystal clear to me.

We turn into the driveway, and as we walk inside, I tamp down the fact that none of us has slept together since I moved in. There have been a few close calls–like when I found Damon sunbathing in the backyard naked, or when Silas and I played footsie under the dining room table.

I still blush when I think of the way he looked at me

over dinner the first night. Like he couldn't believe I was here, like he couldn't wait to devour me.

"Hungry?" Jude murmurs in my ear as Damon closes the door and locks up. He and Silas walk into the house.

They installed a state-of-the-art security system after the other night. And I know they're worried about Liam, and if he's going to go one step further and try to find me—find *us*—here. There has been no news, no arrests, since we filed the police report. Then again, we have no idea which side the police department will take anyway. On paper, we don't look that innocent either.

"Very," I answer, kicking off my sandals and dropping my purse onto the table in the foyer. My eyes scan the wall of crosses, the wall everyone sees first thing when they walk into this house. "Why doesn't Silas take those down?" I ask, crossing my arms.

Jude walks over to the wall and takes one of them off, holding it in his hand. The edges are smooth and long, though the other crosses are all different shapes and sizes. He holds the cross out to me.

"He hasn't changed a single thing since we moved in two years ago. I think he's scared of disturbing the spirits," Jude finishes, chuckling. "Here. Maybe if we take one down at a time, he won't notice."

I shake my head. "I don't want it."

He tilts his head slightly and walks over to me, pinning me against the wall as he brushes the long end of the cross down my chest slowly.

"Don't you?"

My chest rises and falls more rapidly as the smooth edge runs lower, sending shivers down my spine as it teases the sensitive skin between my ribs, and then my belly button, before snagging in the waistband of my pants. He maneuvers it lower, inside the waistband of my pants, and I inhale sharply.

"Jude," I warn, my breath catching as I crane my neck over his shoulder. I don't see Silas or Damon.

He doesn't answer my plea. Instead, he works the button of my pants and unzips them, pulling them low enough to give him access.

"This won't do," he murmurs, scooping me up and carrying me to the foyer table. I gasp as he sets me down and yanks my pants off completely. Clicking his tongue, he takes a step back and admires the sight. "Red panties today."

I swallow my words. My skin is on fire, and I eye the way his strong hands smoothly grip the cross. He can't. He wouldn't–

"Spread your legs, Lennon."

A thrill shoots through me, sending a gush of wetness to the space between my legs. My clit throbs as I scoot back and place my hands behind me, leaning back slightly. My nipples are taut against my t-shirt, and the fabric brushes against them as I wait for Jude to do whatever depraved thing he's going to do. I spread my legs for him, and he groans so low I think I feel him more than hear him.

"That's right, princess," he growls. Moving closer, he takes the cross and runs it up the inside of my left calf.

Slowly.

So *torturously* slowly.

"Jude–"

"Do you want me to stop?" he asks, moving it higher. It's cold, but I'm burning up, so the metal feels amazing against my flushed skin. My whole body convulses, and goosebumps erupt along my skin.

"No," I whisper, my voice pleading. I look down,

analyzing the black cross. The long part is round, smooth, and thick, shaped like a pipe, except it tapers off slightly at the bottom. My eyes flick back up to his, and I spread my legs wider to encourage him.

Jude runs the cross higher, pulling my panties down my legs and discarding them to the side. I hiss as he uses the cross to make slow circles in the area between my thigh and pussy, taunting me.

I move my hands forward and clutch the edge of the table tightly as he spreads my lips with the edge of the cross, playing with them until I drop my head back. Bucking my hips, I wait for him to insert the giant rod.

"What shall I do with this cross?" Jude asks, antagonizing me.

"Just fuck me with it," I answer, my voice uneven and frenzied.

"Do you see how wild you can get for me, Lennon? How crazed I make you?" I whimper, and he runs the cold material up and down my slit, lubing it up with my wetness. "One minute ago, we were walking through the door, and then you gave me an idea with your cross comment," he murmurs, his gold eyes boring into mine. "You drive me wild too, princess," he adds, teasing my entrance. "So fucking unhinged that I'm about to fuck you with this cross."

I gasp as he slowly penetrates me with it. White, blazing heat flares through me at what he's saying—what he's doing.

I move, inching myself lower and lower onto the cross until it's fully sheathed inside of me, stretching me with absolutely no give. God, this thing must be solid metal. It feels heavy, and I can feel my muscles clench around it.

"Fuck," I whisper as he pulls it out, my voice ragged.

When he moves it back in again, he's less gentle, and I hiss again. He groans, biting his lower lip.

"This is so fucking hot," he says quietly. "Lennon Rose fucking a cross. I feel like we should recite the holy sacrament to cancel this whole thing out."

"I don't care," I say unevenly, completely brainless with lust and at his mercy. I'm full on fucking the cross now, undulating my hips. My wetness acts like lube, and he gets rougher. I *need* it rougher.

His eyes go from gold to nearly black, his erection straining against his pants, the sight alone making me moan for more.

He angles the cross ever so differently, hitting me in just the right spot, and a soft whimper leaves me. I begin to quake on the table, causing it to creak. I don't care if Silas sees us—if Damon sees us. I just want to feel myself come around this cross.

"Come for me, Lennon. Come on this cross. And then I'll hang it back up, dripping with your arousal. It can be our little secret."

I cry out as he tilts the cross once again, massaging it against the fleshy spot inside of me, and I explode.

"Fuck!" I groan, my body spasming as wave after wave runs through me, electrifying me. My pussy pulses around the heavy metal rod of the cross, and my eyes roll into the back of my head as my whole body trembles. He made me come all over the cross and the table, so strongly that I can hear it hit the floor, feel it dripping down my legs...

"Good girl," he growls, removing the cross.

Just like he promised, he takes it and hangs it back up on the wall where he found it. It's gleaming with my wetness, and a few drops collect on the bottom. Jude bends down and licks them before standing up and adjusting his pants. Helping me off the table, we both look up at what he did.

"You can't seriously leave it there."

"Oh, I have every intention of leaving it there," Jude growls, grabbing my hand.

I'm still shaking, still panting. He helps me back into my pants, and then we head into the kitchen.

I can't help but look over my shoulder, smiling.

Pretty sure we disturbed more than spirits back there.

three

Lennon

After an amazing meal of the best homemade nachos I've ever had, I stare at my reflection in the guest bathroom down the hallway from my room. For the first time since I left Wright, I feel happier, lighter, more content and secure in myself. I *thought* I was happy before. I *thought* I wanted the Upper East Side lifestyle I'd so perfectly cut out for myself. I constantly told myself that everyone hated button-up shirts and pastel colors, right? It wasn't just me? I assumed we were all just putting on a show for each other. But as I begin to brush my teeth, I realize now that some people are content living that life–and that's fine.

But I wasn't.

Maybe I needed Wright to cheat on me, because by doing so, he saved me from an extremely unhappy situation without even realizing it.

I never had a happy childhood, so how was I supposed to know what *true* happiness felt like? How was I supposed to know that I loved the color black when everyone I knew abhorred it? How was I supposed to glean any insight into myself when all I was doing was presenting myself to Wright in the way *he* wanted me to be? I never realized until this week that all the comments–all the ways he would demean me and bring me down–they took a toll on me. I began to believe them myself.

So when I left and came here, I floundered to find myself. I wasn't sure which way was up those first couple of days.

But Silas, Damon, and Jude gave me something vital.

They gave me stability in the form of a job.

And eventually, they also gave me friendship and trust.

I spit my toothpaste into the sink and rinse out my mouth, quickly washing my face and drying it off. After I rub some lotion in, I turn around and nearly bump into Silas. Living with him–with all of them–has been the epitome of what not to do when you first start dating someone.

And I have three of them to contend with.

Every time they catch me in my ratty pajamas–which is most mornings–and every time I interact with them before I have my coffee, I have to wince. Most women get the chance to dress themselves up and present their best selves to their new beau. Not me. Silas, Damon, and Jude now see me at all hours, every single day. They know what I eat for breakfast. They know I let my dishes sit in the sink all day long. They know I like to spend hours watching trashy television on the weekends. If they looked in my medicine cabinet, they'd see my anxiety medication and the box of super tampons.

Don't even get me started on Damon nearly walking in on me while I was pooping.

"Hey," Silas says, smiling down at me. "I just wanted to say goodnight."

I cross my arms and smirk, biting my lip. "Goodnight."

His eyes scan my bare face. Wright didn't see me without makeup until we moved in together. I used to sleep with it on when I spent the night.

"Is it weird?" he asks, looking down at the floor. "That my brother is also in a relationship with more than one person?"

His question startles me, my brow furrowing. "No. Why would it be weird?"

He shrugs. "It's just unconventional, and the fact that we *both* found more than one partner–"

"Silas," I interrupt, my voice low. "I think you and Ledger had a hell of a childhood. Quite literally. And maybe that means you're making up for it by ensuring you have *extra* love in adulthood."

He grins, his eyes twinkling, and the look warms my chest. "Yeah. I guess you're right. I just didn't want you to think we had a weird fetish or anything. Because of our parents."

"No. I didn't think that, but now I do," I tease, winking as I smile up at him.

He laughs, and then he pulls me into him. I let his arm wrap around my waist, loving the way I feel pressed against him, and his hand trails along the sliver of exposed skin between my tank top and my sleep shorts. His lips find the side of my neck, and I close my eyes and open my mouth in a silent gasp as he kisses me there–sucks on the flesh– before letting me go completely.

My eyes snap open.

"Goodnight, Lennon." His eyes appear darker now than they were a few seconds ago.

I open my mouth to respond, but he turns and leaves the bathroom before I can beg him to stay.

I finish up and walk back down the hallway to my bedroom, pushing the door open and closing it behind me. Leaning against it, I try to contain my smile. As much as I fought against it, I like living here. I enjoy seeing them more often, even if it does mean I have almost no privacy. This feels like a good decision–the *right* decision.

I'm still wired from my strange and erotic encounter with Jude and the cross, so I grab my laptop and begin to draft an email to my mom. I let her know about the apartment the day after it happened, and she sent someone over yesterday to change the locks and fix the place up to rent out. But she didn't say anything else–didn't ask how I was, or if I'd been hurt. I know it's probably futile, but I need to get it all out on paper. I need to tell her exactly how I feel. She may not read it, but every night since the break in, I've jotted down a few pages of thoughts directed at her, and it really helps to calm my mind.

By the time I finish, I feel something akin to contentment for the first time in a long time. Sighing, I turn off my light, climb into bed, and fall asleep.

four

Jude

I sit in the back of the church, waiting for Liam fucking James to make an appearance. The prick really does know how to make a grand entrance, and all his followers eat his holier-than-thou shit right up. They practically froth at the mouth whenever he speaks–whenever he does *anything*. I'm pretty sure he could make a killing selling his dirty socks, and people would buy them for thousands of dollars. Especially the people in Greythorn. Rich and stupid; it's a bad combination, and everyone in this room is both of those things.

Maybe even myself, since I'm here.

Liam finally enters the church, if you can even call it that. It's essentially a recreational room big enough to accommodate a couple hundred people. It's a sad development from what the Church of the Rapture used to be–what the founder of the church used to do. Samuel Kent was the original leader, and he used to hold meetings in a cave about an hour away from here. I'm not into this mumbo-jumbo, but having to pretend in a rural cave seems a hell of a lot more interesting than a place that doubles as a retirement party venue.

Too bad Samuel Kent was just as bad as Liam, if not worse.

Liam begins to speak. I hardly remember when he took over. I was about ten, and while Silas and I were friends, things started to get a lot worse when Liam took the church over from Samuel. More people joined, they moved the church to this building, and they started acting more like a fucking cult than they already had been. There's a good reason Samuel left the church, though–for what he did to Silas. He's been in hiding ever since, and no one knows where he went.

Regardless, every time I attend one of these fucking services, I get creeped the hell out. There's a lot of talk of Jesus descending from the sky, and while no one can tell me when it will happen, they are all convinced it's going to be *soon*. Soon enough to hoard food and act like complete assholes to every other human who may not be holy enough to ascend into Heaven. These people are feral animals. They would throw their children under a bus before they admitted they were drinking the crazy juice. It's a testament to just how impressionable the general public is.

Liam begins to speak about this event, as he always does. His eyes find mine, and like always, they narrow in suspicion as he speaks. I don't give him anything back. My face stays neutral, my arms crossed. I am cautiously interested, or at least, that's the vibe I want to give off. He never approaches me, and I am waiting for the day that he does, so that I can finally start to play the part.

But first, I must put in the work, and that means acting like this is interesting. Showing up every Sunday morning. Looking conflicted and confused.

When Liam finishes, I stand and walk out before the crowd exits. That's another thing–I don't linger. People know me. They see me come inside. That's enough... for now. I hope Liam notices, too. Because one day soon, I'm going to have to pretend I buy into all his bullshit. I'm going to have to become the very thing I hate the most in this world.

five

Lennon

"Wait, wait, wait," Mindy says, shaking her head and nearly dropping the ceramic coffee mug in her hands. "Let me get this straight. You're now dating all *three* of them, *and* you're living with them?" Her brown eyes are wide, and her mouth is open in shock, waiting for me to respond.

I lean back and shrug, trying to hide the giant smile tugging on my lips. "Yeah, I guess so."

She blows out a noisy breath of air. "I mean, save some for the rest of us," she jokes. "Three? All three?"

I laugh. "Yep."

She closes her eyes and places a palm on her forehead. "Please tell me everything before I self-destruct in a fit of envy."

So I do. I tell her everything, except the stuff happening with Liam, and the night we all had sex in front of Wright. One, I don't want to drag her into anything unnecessarily, and two, I don't know if they want anyone else to know about the *other* side of Savage Ink. It's not my secret to tell, so I keep mum on that one aspect of everything that's happened.

When I'm finished, leaving off with the cross, she just closes her eyes and sighs contentedly.

"I mean... I just..." She opens her eyes and leans forward. "You are one lucky bitch, do you know that?"

I laugh again. "I do know." Taking a sip of my cappuccino, I tilt my head. "So, what's new with you?"

She lets out a disgruntled noise. "I mean, things are fine. Just mom things, per usual. I'm certainly not getting rammed by three gorgeous guys at once, though, so..."

"You can borrow them if you want," I joke, and she spits out her coffee.

"Dammit, Lennon." She's still giggling a few minutes later after we've cleaned up the table. She looks over my shoulder at the park, and a sense of peace washes over me.

This–sitting in Greythorn with Mindy–is lovely.

I don't think I want to stay here forever, but right now, it feels gratifying to be home.

"How are the kids?" I ask, taking another sip of my coffee.

She shrugs. "Fine. They're good kids. I'm just exhausted. It's a tough job, but it's also really rewarding. I get to mold little brains all day, every day. It's kind of exciting."

I smile. "Yeah."

Truth be told, I can't stop thinking of Silas holding Easton, and how natural he seemed with a baby. It's not something I expected to see, especially coming from such a giant, scary-looking man.

"Do you want kids?" she asks, her eyes twinkling.

I shrug. "I think so." The answer is out of my mouth

before I can process it. "You know, until a month ago, my default answer was absolutely not. But..." I trail off, playing with the teaspoon next to my coffee mug. "My parents were horrible, so I was never interested in being a parent. But seeing you, and my friend Lola..." I shake my head. "I'm not sure anymore, but I'm leaning toward yes."

She nods. "I think your fears are valid, though. My parents were great, but I still had my doubts. I didn't expect to get pregnant so young, but I think I'm a good mom, so it worked out. I was meant to do this."

I nod. "You're a natural."

"Don't get me wrong, the little shits really piss me off on a daily basis," she adds, and I laugh. "But the good outweighs the bad." She swirls her coffee around in her mug. "I think it also takes meeting the right person." She looks up at me. "I mean, you remember what I was like in high school. Gabriel met me when I was like *that*, but he still managed to sweep me off my feet. People liked to talk shit since he was older, but you know what? It felt like the puzzle pieces of my life finally came together when I met him."

I pretend to gag, and she laughs. "I'm mostly joking. You guys are wonderful together, and it's obvious it was meant to be. I mean... ten years, three kids..."

"Maybe four," Mindy muses, and my eyes go wide.

"Four? But that's double the number of adults!"

She cackles. "I know, I know. But watching Gabriel be a dad—and he's such a good dad—is addicting." She quirks an eyebrow. "You'll see one day."

I sigh. "You're getting ahead of yourself."

"Nope. One day, something will just click, and boom, baby fever."

I quell the excited butterflies that flit through me. In the future–*way* in the future. I still need to get my feet on the ground, find my own place to live, start baking again, perhaps even open a bakery…

Mindy seems to read my mind. "You know, a friend of a friend of a friend let me know about this space down the street. It'll be available for rent in three months." She smirks and leans back, pulling one leg under her as she cups her mug. "Gabriel knows of an investment banker. We could shoot the shit with him and see if we can pull some strings."

I'd told her about my dream of opening a bakery before, and the last time we met up for coffee, I'd mentioned it again. Looking down, more nervous butterflies fly around my stomach, and I set my coffee down, suddenly overwhelmed by the prospect of everything that would entail.

"Let me get my bearings a bit," I respond, my voice soft. "It's barely been a month. I don't want to make any rash decisions."

Mindy shrugs. "I understand. When you're ready, just let me know."

I think of it–of a cute place here with checkered curtains, scones and coffee, baking side by side with Lola, Betsy the mixer on display as a show of how far I've come…

It's jolting how quickly I've become attached to the new image of my potential future, and I grab the table to steady myself a bit. Not only was my life turned upside down just weeks ago, but I'm now dating and living with three men whom I barely know–not really, anyway. There's a psychotic cult leader out to get me, and I still need to figure out my life and what I want to do. I'm not even sure I want to stay in Greythorn–though Mindy, Lola, and the guys are a good incentive to stay.

Silas's words from the day we went to view the condo pop into my head.

I know your soul died the instant you came back here. I don't want to see the fire inside of you go out forever because you got stuck.

I know this isn't their dream, either, and that brings me some semblance of comfort. The future is limitless, and the endless possibilities are terrifying for someone who thought she knew exactly how her life would go after college graduation.

A few minutes later, I say goodbye to Mindy and walk back to the car that Silas lent me. I try to quell the shivers that break out along my skin every time I get into the black Lexus sedan. I know his parents murdered someone, but I'm too chicken to ask if this car was involved. Just using the same car they did–with all the normal things a car has, like their sunglasses–gives me the creeps. That said, I am grateful they lent it to me, as having a bit of autonomy feels nice.

I could find happiness here if I had to.

I'm just not sure I want to settle down in the place that always brought me so much grief.

six

Lennon

I get home just as the guys come up from working out in the basement gym, which is in the other part of the basement from the chapel. Every time they come upstairs into the kitchen, I think I've gotten used to three brutal, giant shirtless men dripping with sweat, all pumped up with adrenaline from lifting weights. I think I've finally come to terms with the fact that these men are my friends, and now more than that, that we all share something I've never experienced with anyone else before. And then as Silas goes upstairs to shower and Jude answers a phone call, walking out of the room, Damon pins me with a heated expression—his dark, scythe eyebrows moving together as he asks a silent question. His chin-length hair is pulled back into a bun, and his scruff is dripping with sweat. His thick, sculpted abdomen contracts with every movement, and his dark gray sweatpants leave nothing to the imagination, either. He cocks his head to the side and stalks toward me slowly.

Like a predator waiting to pounce.

No, I am never going to get used to this.

"How's Mindy?" Damon asks, his voice distracted and faraway. Like he's making small talk before he devours me whole.

I swallow, my eyes meeting his as he stops a few inches from me. My chest rises and falls as my breathing turns ragged.

"She's good," I answer, digesting his words. I always forget they know her from Ravenwood Academy. It's surreal to think these giants before me have been in my life for nearly twenty years. It brings me an odd sense of familiarity. We know the same people, and we frequent the same spots. All four of us are products of this fucked up little suburb. It makes me feel like we have some sort of camaraderie, besides the obvious sexual tension.

"Having a nice morning?" he asks, inching closer, his warmth enveloping me and making my heart pick up its pace.

I nod my head vigorously. "Yeah. I was thinking of going–"

"That's good," he interrupts, placing a finger underneath my chin. I can smell his sweat–the potent, heady smell that makes my knees weak. It's all *man*, and it drives me fucking insane every time I breathe it in. "Why don't we go upstairs? I need help cleaning myself off," he purrs, his voice soft and low all at once–like liquid velvet.

Fuck.

"Okay," I whisper, turning around and walking up the stairs.

Four weeks ago, I would've slapped any man that commanded me the way Damon does. He's always in control, always playing the part of a true alpha male. I was never attracted to that, but then again, I'd never experienced a man like Damon before. But now? I'd bend over and let him do whatever the fuck he wanted with me–with any part of me. In fact, I'm pretty sure the same can be said for all three of them. They have me completely at their beck and call, wrapped around their fingers. As I ascend the stairs and walk into Damon's ensuite bathroom, I'm starting to realize how much they can control me with just a single look or word.

When I turn around, Damon unties his pants and doesn't take his eyes off me as he pulls them down over his large erection. My throat goes dry for a second when I realize I let *that thing* in my ass not too long ago. Without hesitating, I strip out of my leggings and t-shirt, leaving me in my turquoise underwear and matching bra.

"You're a big boy," I tease, running my finger up and down my bra strap. "Why do you need help showering?" I tilt my head to the side, knowing from the way his eyes narrow ever so slightly that he knows I'm taunting him. Maybe I'm doing it on purpose, or maybe I'm giving myself a bit of time to calm my racing heart. I don't know if I'll ever get used to sleeping with any of them. It's been a religious experience every time, and I've never been with Damon alone. He's the most feral of them all.

A beast, ready to dominate.

I can't help but get a little excited at the prospect of riling him up before he has his way with me.

He drops his eyes to my legs, slowly trailing up them again. When his irises meet mine, they're pure black, and he fists his palms at his sides. I fully expect him to bust out of his skin and turn into the hulk. My breath catches in my throat, and I stand up straighter. My clit throbs as I bend down to get my clothes, seeing how far I can push him.

"Well, if you don't need my help anymore, I'll just be on my w—"

Before I can get the last word out, he rushes toward me, shooting a hand out and grabbing me by my underwear. Pulling roughly, he rips it off me, and then he reaches up and fists my hair. He's not gentle, and he's not nice. I'm nearly gasping for air as he pushes me backward into the large shower. I open my mouth to speak, but he clamps his large palm over my lips as the other hand unclasps my bra, letting it fall to the ground. Lowering his forehead, he removes his hand and then smashes his lips against mine.

His tongue swoops into my mouth, overtaking me. His other hand continues to fist the back of my hair, pulling my face closer and then pulling it away as his lips graze my jaw, my neck, my collarbone...

I gasp as his teeth close around my nipple, and he bites—hard enough for me to yelp. The sound causes him to flip me around so that my face is against the cold marble of the shower, and I turn my cheek and watch as he strokes his cock behind me. I can't help but whimper as his hand runs along my ass cheek. I like this—the no talking, the animalistic need to have him. Without warning, two fingers dip between my legs and tease my wet entrance. Damon groans with satisfaction, and then he slides one finger inside of me.

"Fuck," I whisper, bucking my hips against his hand. At that word, he inserts a second finger. I moan, closing my eyes. He growls as he fucks me with his hand, and the hard ridge of his cock thrusts against my ass. My whole body is on fire, and I cry out against the stone as his fingers curve, hitting the perfect spot. My knees buckle and he rubs himself against me faster and faster, fucking me but not really fucking me.

"Damon," I plead, my voice uneven and raw.

My words cause him to pull his fingers out, and the next thing I know, he's knocking my knees apart and pulling my hips closer to him. I gasp as the head of his thick shaft rubs against my wetness. Grunting, he thrusts into me, and I lose myself in him–in the heady smell of him, the feel of his smooth length, the way his calloused hands come up and around to twist my nipples. One of his hands edges lower, yanking my hips into him so that I'm fucking his cock instead of the other way around. I cry out, my whole body beginning to shake as he quickens his pace.

Feral sounds are leaving us with each thrust, moans and groans, wet, slapping noises, and his movements get more frantic as he continues to fuck me against the wall of the shower.

Is it possible to die from too much pleasure? When it becomes too much that it's almost painful? I'm going to shoot up into the ceiling soon. I whimper as Damon pulls out of me, and when I turn around, he's watching me with a monstrous grin.

seven

Damon

Lennon's pussy is made of warm, soft velvet–and it's like everything about her was created for me. Her sizable tits with perfect, round, pink nipples. Her long, blonde hair that falls down her back. Her legs–*fuck*, her legs. Long, slender, toned. And her mouth? *Fuck*. I fucking love her heart-shaped mouth.

I turn the shower on and hoist her up so that she's wrapped around my waist. The bathroom instantly gets steamy. She slides against me, and I press her against the wall with the showerhead, the water running down between our bodies. Moaning, she bucks against me, searching for friction, nipping at my neck like a savage little beast. I let out a low laugh as I press my throbbing cock back inside of her, and I groan when I feel her clench around me.

"You like that?" I ask, thrusting into her roughly. I

should probably be gentler, should probably have warmed her up a bit, but something about my workout today and seeing her in *my* kitchen turned me into an animal.

"God, yes," she whimpers, making a keening noise in the back of her throat. "Harder."

I grin. "I'm not sure how much rougher I can go," I muse, clenching my jaw as I slam into her.

Her cries echo loudly against the marble, and I feel my balls tighten.

"Come on, Brooks. Give it to me."

I let out a surprised laugh as I pull out and forcefully drive into her repeatedly. Her eyes roll into the back of her head. She's in a taunting mood today, teasing me to fire me up. *Fine.* I hold on to her ass with one hand as she writhes into me, and I use the other hand to slap her clit–*hard.*

"Fuck!" she cries, bucking against me. I feel her pussy feather around my rock-hard shaft, milking it up and down in a way that makes me close my eyes and gasp.

I roughly flick her clit again, and she loses it on top of me. Bleating like a lamb, she twitches as her pussy contracts around me, and I feel myself spill into her as I roar.

"Fuck, Damon," she hisses, her eyes squeezed shut as my cock pulses into her. Sagging against me, we stay there for a minute, catching our breath as the water flows between us.

I gently set her down, and then, without another word, pull her into the shower stream with me. We take turns washing each other, and I take special care with the shampoo, making sure I give her a good scalp massage. She moans against me, and my cock hardens again instantly. Smirking, she flings water in my face as she rinses off.

When we're done, I wrap her in one of my towels and

carry her to my room. I thought we were done, but the way my dick reacts around her tells me that I'm *not* done. Pressing gentle kisses against her raw lips, I reach down and slowly insert myself inside of her.

She gasps. "Again?"

I kiss her again, chuckling. "I could probably go a third time, too, if you wanted."

"My vagina is going to fall off," she says weakly, her hands gripping onto me as I pull out slowly before thrusting back in.

"Doubtful." I nip at her ear, and she groans as I push in all the way to the hilt, filling her completely. I reach down and begin stroking her clit, smiling when I feel her contract around me with every movement. She's like a ticking time bomb–and she comes so hard. How her ex never made her come is beyond me, but I'm more than happy to ply her with multiple orgasms.

"Come for me, Lennon," I demand, quickening my pace.

"Oh God, I'm–" She arches her back as she flies off the bed, screaming my name.

"That's it." I thrust into her and hold her legs wide as she milks my cock, her body shaking. *Fuck. Me.* "Fuck, you're going to make me come," I add, my voice hoarse. "Just looking at your pretty, little pussy squeeze my cock, fuck." The room spins in the best way possible. "Watch me fill you until you're overflowing with my come, Lennon."

She whimpers as I fill her, roaring. My cock bobs inside of her, each wave shooting come that spills out of her. My hands tremble as I hold her legs up, and when I finish coming, I dip my head and try to catch my breath.

Falling to the bed next to her, we both stare up at the ceiling.

"Want to try for a third?" she asks, her voice casual and light.

I could fucking marry this woman.

eight

Lennon

"Stay still," Silas orders, holding me down on his tattoo chair. "I promise it won't hurt that much."

I roll my eyes. "Yes, and your nose ring looks so amazing, Silas Huxley," I say sarcastically.

He chuckles, holding a needle that looks *way* too big to be going through my delicate nostril.

"Relax, Lennon. We can stop any time."

I narrow my eyes. "No. It's fine. I just have a thing with my nose. But I've always wanted a nose ring, so let's do it."

"Want a drink?" Jude asks from across the studio.

I shake my head. "No." I wipe my palms on my skirt and lay back down. "Just do it. I'll close my eyes. Don't tell me when you're close."

It's five minutes to opening, and I decided spontaneously about twenty minutes ago to get a nose piercing. I wanted one in high school, but I never got around to doing it. In college, Wright always looked down on tattoos and piercings, so I never had the chance with him. I squeeze my eyes shut and clench my fists tightly, waiting.

I hear him move closer, whimpering as the needle goes through my nostril. It really fucking hurts. My eyes water, and I feel tears drip down my cheeks as he tugs a bit on the sensitive skin. The stinging gives way to throbbing, and I feel like I'll never be able to open my eyes.

"All done," he says proudly, holding a mirror up.

I force my eyes open, wiping my cheeks. I opted for a simple diamond stud, and I immediately love the way it looks. Wiggling my nose a tad, I smile up at him.

"That wasn't so bad."

"Just promise me you'll let me do your nipples," Jude chimes in from his station.

"I get your cunt," Damon adds just as the first customer walks in.

I have to stifle my laugh.

It takes a couple of hours for the pain to subside, but it does, eventually. As long as I don't accidentally touch the piercing, I hardly notice it's there. I'm just getting Jude's third client checked in when Lola struts in.

"Well, surprise, surprise," I muse, standing up and giving her a big hug. "How are you?"

She grins and takes a step back. Dressed impeccably in black ripped jeans and a white tank top that perfectly matches her white chucks, she flails her arms out to the side.

"I found a space for the bakery," she squeals, and I hear Silas clap for her from his place at his station.

My mouth pops open. "Oh my God, that's amazing!"

She nods. "Yeah. It's *perfect,* Lennon. It's on the corner, down a few blocks," she adds, gesturing outside. "I know I said I wanted to be in Boston, but this is where our life is right now, so why wait? Large kitchen, enough space for people to eat in and have a coffee..." she trails off and places her hands on her cheeks. "I signed the lease even though I have zero money to my name. I had to."

"That's so exciting! Do you need help with anything–"

"Lennon," she cuts me off, sternly, her face lighting up as she stares me down. "I want you there with me."

The chatter happening in the back quiets, and I know the guys are listening in now.

"What? Really?"

She nods vigorously. "Yes. I need you there by my side. And I tried one of your cupcakes the other day," she adds, referencing the party at the house on Sunday. "You might be a better baker than me. How do you get your buttercream *so* soft? And it's not too sweet, either. I've never tasted frosting like that before."

I smirk. "I add milk. And *lots* of butter–salted. Just be sure to keep it refrigerated, because it melts easily."

She smacks the desk. "Ah! I knew it had to be dairy. That's genius." She takes my hands. "Please. Please do this with me."

I twist my lips to the side. On the one hand, I want to scream *yes!* But on the other hand, I can't help but feel like I don't want to establish roots here, because I don't plan on staying.

"Can I think about it and let you know tomorrow?" I ask, gripping her hands tightly.

"Of course. I just wanted to tell you and offer you a co-partnership. *If* you're interested. By the way, I love the nose piercing." She wiggles her eyebrows and then walks into the back to say hi to the guys. My hands are still limp at my sides as I digest her words.

A bakery–here in Greythorn. Working with Lola, doing what I love...

It could be great.

So why am I not jumping for joy?

Lola leaves soon after, and the four of us finish up our shift in perfect harmony. Now that I've been here for a few weeks, we've gotten into a rhythm at the end of the night. Each guy cleans his station–sanitizing, organizing, and getting it ready for the next day. Even though they clean before each client, they take health and safety very seriously. I finish up whatever tasks and emails that are outstanding. Since I spend most of the night behind the computer and checking clients in, I usually get everything done before we close at two. I check the client list for the next day, skimming the names so that I know who to expect, and if it's a repeat customer, I let the guys know so they can review their past work and refresh their memories. I also schedule a few social media posts, quickly tidy the bathroom, and make sure the place looks nice for when we re-open.

Some nights, the guys turn down the lights and kick back on the couch, beers in hand. My eyes usually get heavy by this point, and most nights, I end up dozing on someone's shoulder, but I know they need to decompress and come down from creating all night. Tonight, though, we're headed straight home. I'm exhausted from my afternoon with Damon, and Jude is tired from spending the morning at church.

He still won't tell me why he's there and what he plans to do. He just keeps telling us that consistency is key, and he needs to make Liam believe he's genuinely curious. We turn out the lights and head out, and I lock the door as Silas waits with me. Jude and Damon head to Damon's car a couple of blocks away. Now that summer is in full swing, Greythorn is getting more tourists, which means we've had a harder time finding parking close to Savage Ink. Silas wraps an arm around my shoulder as we walk a couple hundred feet behind Jude and Damon. I'm just about to ask what he's going to make us for a midnight snack when he stops, tugging me into his side.

"Well, well, well," a voice drawls from the darkness to our left.

My eyes flick to the alley, and to my horror, Liam steps out, cigarette in hand.

"Those things will kill you," Silas drawls, his voice composed.

Liam shrugs. "I'm not worried. The best part of my life happens after I die."

Shivers run down my spine at his words. He is so convinced the rapture is happening–so convinced he will be saved. I didn't grow up religious, so the thought of devoting my life to something like that... I can't fathom it. To harm people because the afterlife is going to save you? It feels a little fucked up to me. I'm all for helping people with religion, for bettering the world. But Silas's parents were a part of the Church of the Rapture. They *killed* someone. And Liam broke into my apartment.

None of that seems holy to me.

"What if you're wrong?" I ask, my voice louder than I anticipated. "About the rapture–about all of it? What if you die and it's just all blackness, and–"

Liam chuckles and takes a step forward into the light. He flicks his cigarette onto the sidewalk, and he doesn't even have the audacity to put it out with his shoe.

"Not possible," Liam says slowly. "God talks to me."

Another shiver. This guy is *totally* unhinged. Silas grips

my shoulder a little harder the closer Liam gets. I see Jude and Damon quickly turning around and walking toward us.

"I'm actually not here for either of you," Liam adds, cocking his head. Jude and Damon stop a few feet from me, and both stand with their legs apart in a protective manner. "I'm here for him." He nods to Jude.

No.

"The fuck you are," Damon spits. He looks at Jude. "Let's go."

"Well, this is awkward," Liam drawls, sauntering up to Jude, who just clenches his jaw as Liam pops an arm around his shoulder. "Should you tell them, or shall I?"

Jude's nostrils flare, and panic fills me. He looks up at Silas then, a pleading look on his face.

"I–I've been going to a few of the meetings," he says quickly, and I hide my relieved expression.

This is a game.

We're playing a game, that's all.

"You've *what*?" Silas spits, releasing me in a show of pure shock. I'm impressed. Had I not been in on the secret, this would all seem genuine to me.

"How could you?" I whisper, just for show.

Jude shrugs. "I went as a joke at first, but then I started to… kind of like it. I don't participate," he adds, looking at Silas. "I just observe."

Of course, we know this, but as I look over at Liam's wicked grin, I realize this is exactly the kind of reaction they'd expected.

And this is exactly the kind of ambush they wanted from Liam.

"Let's go," Liam says gruffly. "Unless you're not really serious?" he taunts, his face inches from Jude, who is stiff as a rod.

"You're not going anywhere with this bastard," Damon growls at Jude.

Liam chuckles. "Calm down, Brooks. I'm just taking him for a beer at The Queens Arms."

"It's closed," Silas says quickly, a hint of relief in his voice.

Maybe I should nominate the three of them for an Oscar.

"Not for me," Liam answers, holding out a key,

My stomach twists. I know this is a game, and it's all for show, but I don't like the idea of Jude being alone with Liam. What if they know we're messing with them and his guys ambush Jude? I don't know the details of Silas's parent's murder, but if Liam was behind that...

"Don't go," I say quickly. I'm not really pretending this time.

Jude must sense the change in my tone, because he quirks a smile and winks at me.

"Don't worry, princess. Just one drink. And then I'll be home to tuck you in."

I clench my jaw as Liam leads Jude away, and I can't help the weird, achy feeling in my chest. I put a hand on my neck as I watch them go. Once they're far enough away, I spin around to Silas.

"You're just going to let him go?" I ask.

"Lennon—"

"No." My voice is hushed now so that we don't draw attention to ourselves. Damon and Silas usher me toward the car. "I know you were all faking that performance," I start, and Damon laughs.

"Was it that obvious?"

I glare at him as we walk up to the shiny silver BMW. Damon's car. It's oddly neutral for such a big personality.

"You know what I mean. But what if Jude gets hurt in there? We all know how deranged Liam is."

Silas sighs as he opens the passenger door for me. "Jude can handle himself. I promise."

Once the doors are closed, I turn around to face Silas, who is on his phone.

"Look," he says, showing me a map on his screen. "Jude asked that I track him for safety purposes a few weeks ago, right when he started attending the services. If anything funny happens, I'll call the police."

I scowl, ignoring the tiny bit of relief that brings me. They could always stash his phone somewhere, or break it, or–

"Baby girl." Damon speaks to me gently, reaching for my hand. "I can assure you; Jude will be fine. They're just trying to gauge his interest. They want to feel him out. We planned for this. *Anticipated* it. It's what they do. We've been watching Liam for a very long time."

I nod slowly. "Fine." I cross my arms and then I look back at Silas. "Now, tell me about the person your parents murdered."

nine

Jude

I watch as the condensation from the beer slides down the side of the pint glass, and I use my finger to stop it before it leaves a ring on the dingy wooden bar table. Liam hasn't stopped talking since we sat down. I can tell it's been a long time since they had a new recruit. The murder got a lot of bad press, as did the church. Still, the motherfucker is on a roll, trying to sell his dying religion to a man more sinful than the devil himself. After all, I'm his worst nightmare.

I nod when appropriate, laugh when prompted... and when he's finished spewing his holy vitriol, I sigh and lean back against the bar stool in a show of conflicting interests.

It will be easy to make this believable.

But I'm going to loathe every fucking second of it.

"You can see why I have my hesitations," I say, my voice light, casual. The overhead lights are dim, and it's just the two of us in here. Truthfully, I don't know who would win in a fight, and that thought unsettles me. I'm better at mind games, but Liam is a monster physically. "I grew up with Silas. I watched his parents descend into madness over this church. Why should I join when there are other religious outlets for me?"

Liam smirks, setting his empty beer glass down. "Let me turn your own question back around at you. Why attend our service over another church?"

I look over his shoulder, focusing on the wood-paneled walls. I've always hated this pub. Maybe it's because my dad spent more time here than he did at home, or maybe it's because we figured out the Church of the Rapture owned it a few years ago. Either way, it was a disgrace of a pub, and my skin itched every second we sat in here.

"I'm curious..." I say slowly. "About the afterlife." I play with the condensation on my glass a bit more. *Make it look like I'm nervous; uncomfortable. Make him believe I'm having second thoughts with my body language.* "I've never been one to believe things just end–poof, blackness," I drawl, smiling. I make a show of it and let my hand shake slightly. I don't miss the way Liam's eyes flick downward. "I like the idea of knowing there's something waiting for me. The world is a fucked-up place, Liam. I want a guarantee that I will be rewarded when this is all over." Liam's lips curve upward.

It's in the bag.

I'd researched, listened to interviews with religious zealots. I wanted to study why they acted the way they did, and it all came down to greed. There was no Christ left in these people. They wanted gold and puppies and Range Rovers in Heaven. They weren't satisfied with the life they had here.

They wanted *more*.

Thought they deserved *more*.

It's a dark place to be mentally, but it seems to work, because Liam shakes his head and lets out a loud breath of air.

"Fuck, Vanderbilt. I was sure you were still fucking with me. You really want to be here?"

No.

"Yes," I answer, my voice wavering just a bit. "But I need you to promise me something," I add, furrowing my brows. "You leave my friends alone. This is my decision, and in time, they will come to respect it. So, I need you back the fuck off us, and especially Lennon."

Liam smirks and crosses his arms. "You know I will."

No, you fucking won't.

I know he's lying. But this places me in the perfect position of being on both sides. As Liam tells me a bit more about the church, I sit diligently. This will be my life now, whether I like it or not. *Pretending.* I need to straddle the line between Silas, Damon, Lennon, and the church. I need Liam to see me struggle in real time. And when that struggle becomes too much? I will come to him, and I will pretend I'm all in. And once he shares his fucked-up plans, which will surely involve them, I can relay them to my friends.

We will always be one step ahead.

After all, this is all for them.

For Silas, Damon, and Lennon.

ten

Lennon

I sit and wait for Silas to explain, arms crossed, as we sit in downtown Greythorn, in Damon's car, at three in the morning. My eyebrows quirk up as he sighs, running his hands through his hair. My gaze keeps darting to The Queens Arms a couple of blocks away, waiting to see a bunch of thugs enter to beat Jude up. But I trust Damon and Silas, and I trust that they wouldn't let anything happen to their best friend. I know Jude can handle himself, but the whole thing still makes me nervous now that I know how crazy Liam really is.

"Fine, but I promise it's not as interesting as you're hoping."

I roll my eyes. "I'll be the judge of that."

His nostrils flare as he rubs his lips with his hand, looking down at the floor of the car.

"Growing up, my parents had this friend named Oliver. He

was a young member of the church. Easily Influenced. They had him do all their dirty work." His eyebrows bunch together. "Samuel Kent was the founder of the church, and then Liam took over. For years, it was my parents and Liam, but there were rumors that Liam and Oliver didn't get along. Oliver left the church about three years ago and started causing problems. He had a bunch of recordings from services, and he basically threatened to turn everything over to the FBI. Liam didn't like that and ordered my parents to kill him."

He shrugs. "They were so deep in this bullshit that they did it. They couldn't see right from wrong. He was a sinner, and the world was going to be a better place without him. One night, they drove to his house outside of Boston, and they shot him. I'm still not sure who pulled the trigger. They never admitted which one of them did it. We moved back for the trial, Liam got them the plea deal, and they've been locked up ever since."

I sigh. "Fuck. Liam *ordered* them to kill Oliver?"

"We think so," Damon adds from the back. "Like I said before, nothing has ever been proven. No motive, nothing. Someone scrubbed Oliver's hard drive, cell phone, house, you name it."

"That's super suspicious," I remark slowly. "The judge—" I pause, remembering. "Oh. I remember you mentioning that the judge was a member of the church." Chills spider-walk down my spine.

"The media wasn't that interested after the sentencing, and we've been here ever since, living in their fucked-up house," Damon explains, his voice rough. "We know what they did, but we can't prove shit. Hence why Jude is undercover."

"And how do we know they won't kill Jude for this?" I

whisper, looking in the direction of The Queens Arms. "If they find out he's pretending?"

"Because we're going to finish what Oliver started before they can lay a finger on him. And because Jude is a badass, and he would never let them know he's playing them. There are things that go way back, Lennon. Back to Samuel Kent." He glances at Silas, and they share a quick look. "Pedophilia, drug peddling, money laundering... you name it."

I nod, swallowing. "The tattoos. The rivalry. The break in. I get it now. Liam is dangerous."

"It's why we wanted you living with us. Nowhere is going to be one-hundred percent safe, but at least you have us. And a really fucking expensive security system."

"That doesn't have a visible camera," Silas adds. "It's why Liam was able to get into your apartment. The bastard knew where the camera was and destroyed it that night."

I sit up straighter. "Wait, do you think Liam saw what–what happened that night?"

Damon shrugs. "Fuck if I care."

My skin goes cold at the thought of Liam James watching us all have sex.

"I'm still not sure why he hates you so much." Damon and Silas share a look, and I sigh. "Great. What other super-secret, super creepy secret are you keeping from me?"

"About three years ago, before Oliver was murdered, I was visiting my parents in Greythorn. Liam was over, and he stayed late, past when they went to sleep," Silas starts, his nostrils flaring. "I was just about to head to bed. For a long time, he was a family friend. I never cared for him, but I grew up with him around. That night, he kissed me. Cupped my cock. His intentions were *very* clear."

I rear my head back. "Oh, he's attracted to men?"

Damon shakes his head. "Not publicly. If something like that ever got out..." he pauses, letting out a loud breath of air through his lips. "The church prides themselves on marriage only between a man and a woman."

I shrug. "Okay. He's not the first person to tout that while also being a huge hypocrite."

Silas opens his mouth and smiles. "I have footage of him. Of us. Of me rejecting him."

I groan. "Of course you do."

"He's afraid I'm going to out him," Silas adds.

I frown. "Are you?"

He shrugs, taking a deep breath. "I threatened him when my parents got arrested. I knew he was behind it. So, the option is always on the table. I don't want to resort to that. I'd rather find something having to do with the business of the church. I'm not about outing someone who isn't ready to be outed, no matter how much of a fucking dick they are."

"So, you're sending Jude into the pit instead of just showing everyone the footage of him coming onto you?"

Silas sighs, seeing that I'm getting more upset, and Damon reaches over to hold my hand, his thumb rubbing back and forth soothingly to try to calm me down. "What would that do? Sure, it would crush Liam. But the church would find another leader. They'd continue preying on innocent people, doing shady things, and people's lives might be in danger. I want to find something to take the whole thing down–something to make the members scatter like cockroaches. Liam hates me because I rejected him, and because I have footage of him committing a sin. But I hate the whole damn organization, and I want them all to burn to the ground."

He's breathing heavily, and I realize that this–all of

this—the revenge plot, the anger, the hatred... it's personal for him.

The church stole his parents from him.

The church ruined his childhood, and he wasn't going to let it ruin the rest of his life.

He continues. "Him breaking into your apartment was the last fucking straw, Lennon. They are dead to me. Every single one of them. I told Jude to find something to obliterate them all." He glances at Damon, and even though I think there's something else they're not telling me, I don't ask questions.

I place a hand on his knee. "I understand. And I wholeheartedly support you. I hope you know that," I say softly.

He moves his hand on top of mine. "I know. And we'll get them." Damon's hand comes around to Silas's shoulder from the back, squeezing once. "And I promise, Jude will be fine. Let's head home and get something to eat."

I nod, squeezing his leg before he turns the ignition on, and we head back to the house.

eleven

Silas

None of us speaks as we get back to the house. When I look over at Lennon, she has a worried scowl on her face, and Damon just looks pissed off, as always. I grind my jaw as I heat up some leftover pasta for all of us. This is our ritual—we eat a late lunch before people arrive in the studio, and then we eat again when we get home. I like to cook, so that usually falls on me, though Lennon oversees the baking. My pants are definitely tighter since she moved in.

Lennon is checked out in front of the TV when I bring her a bowl of pasta Bolognese. Damon devours two bowls and I go back for seconds, and still, Jude doesn't come home. I know they're both going to wait up for him.

And I will, too.

I turn the reality show off and slap my hands on my thighs, standing. "Alright, we need to do something productive until Jude comes home. We can't just stew in our anxiety."

Lennon frowns. "Have you checked his location?"

I show her Jude's blue dot. Still at The Queen's Arms. "He's fine. Just playing his game." I take her hands. "I'm worried, too. This whole thing is super fucked. He's taking one for the team, but he's the only one Liam would believe could ever cross over to the dark side."

She sniffs, and Damon scoots closer to her. "Jude will fuck him up if anything fishy happens. Don't worry about him." He puts a hand on Lennon's shoulder, and I see the tension begin to melt away as she closes her eyes and rolls her neck. He begins to massage her flesh, and she groans.

"Oh my God, I didn't realize how tense I was."

Damon growls. "Lie down on the couch, princess."

She snaps her eyes open and looks between the two of us. I raise my eyebrows and Damon just smiles mischievously.

"I think I know where this is going," she murmurs.

"You wanted a distraction," I add, smirking.

She scowls but doesn't say anything as she lies down on the massive couch in our sitting room. We weren't allowed to eat in here growing up, but since I moved back and put a TV in, we spend most of our meals in this casual room off the kitchen. Lennon stands up and orients herself on the couch, lying down on her stomach with her arms above her head. Damon kneels, reaching over and rubbing both shoulders vigorously.

The noises coming from Lennon's throat make me hard instantly.

"Princess," I warn, my voice low, "if you keep making noises like that, I'm going to want to fuck you."

Damon hums in agreement, and Lennon turns her head so that she's looking straight at me. I can already tell from her hooded lids that she's about to damn us with her next sentence.

"So do it."

Sometimes, she's so fucking blunt, and I swear I feel my cock strain against my jeans when her eyes dip to my bulge.

Damon looks over at me and shrugs. "It's not like it'll be the first time."

I smile, and Lennon's eyes flit between us. "Have you guys ever..." she trails off.

Damon clears his throat. "Jude and I fool around sometimes, when we've had too much to drink."

His confession doesn't surprise me. I knew it happened sometimes. Didn't change a thing. I'd always considered myself completely straight, but I was willing to try anything once. Damon is like a brother to me, and like he said, it wouldn't be the first time.

My cock jumps again when I remember Lennon sucking me off while Jude and Damon fucked her.

"Could you show me?" she asks, twisting and turning to her side. "Please."

The way she bites her lower lip, pulling it into her mouth...

I look at Damon, and he tilts his head. "You want a piece of this man meat, Huxley?"

Lennon giggles, but I don't say anything as I walk over to Damon–still on his knees–and begin to unzip my pants.

"Suck it, Brooks."

I love the sound of Lennon's sharp inhale. Damon doesn't miss a beat as he grunts, grabbing my hips and pulling me closer. Perhaps I'm taking advantage. I know he's bi. And maybe I'm curious about what it would feel like to have a man suck my cock. I trust him, and if I was going to experiment with anything, I would want it to be with my best friends. There's something about going through trauma with someone. Even something like this doesn't pose a risk to our friendship. It's solid—and a blowjob won't change anything.

Damon glares up at me before grabbing my shaft. I hiss as his large, warm hand begins to stroke me.

"Nice dick," he remarks, his voice gravelly, before taking me fully into his mouth and to the back of his throat.

I reach out for something to hold on to as the shock and sensation runs through me. I swear out loud and buck my hips as Damon's large tongue swirls around the head of my erection. His mouth is bigger than I'm used to, and he's able to take me to the hilt, swallowing me and using his strength to jerk me off at the same time. His other hand comes to my balls, cupping them gently. There's something to be said for getting your cock sucked by another man. They know how to handle it.

"Fuck," I whisper, running a hand through my hair. I look over at Lennon, and she's watching us raptly. "You like this, princess?" I ask, my voice uneven.

"Fuck yeah," she breathes out, and her hand runs down to her waistband.

twelve

Lennon

My hands find my clit, frenzied and desperate. I don't think I've ever seen anything so hot. Silas writhes into Damon's mouth, and watching the trust, the *love* between them... it's amazing. Silas hisses again, thrusting himself forward. My fingers circle my swollen nub, and I moan.

Silas's gaze finds mine. His eyes are dark now, and his jaw clenched. I sit up and take my pants off, leaning back against the couch and spreading my legs. My hand works faster as Damon ups his tempo, taking Silas in fully before pulling off.

"Does this make you want to fuck us?" Damon asks, looking at me.

"Yes," I whisper. I can't help the desperation in my voice.

Damon chuckles and stands up. "I'll be right back. Get naked."

He leaves Silas and me alone, and I look over at him. We

watch each other as we undress. My chest rises and falls as Silas kicks his pants off and starts to stroke his massive cock. He walks over to me, reaching out and sliding a finger down my wet slit.

"Fuck, Lennon." He rubs the head of his cock against my wetness. "I could come just by touching you." I spread my legs and throw my head back as his soft cock teases my clit, slapping it a few times. "I love how fucking wet you get for us."

"Well, that was the hottest thing I think I've ever seen."

He gives me a lopsided smile. "Noted."

Before I can respond, Damon is back with a bottle of lube. "Let's go up to my bedroom," he commands, looking at me.

I don't say anything as the three of us head upstairs. When Damon closes the door behind him, I pull my arms around myself.

"Is that for me?" I ask, pointing to the bottle. My body sparks at the thought of feeling both inside of me.

Damon looks at Silas as he takes his clothes off. "I was thinking I could fuck Silas while he fucked you."

Silas furrows his brows. "Do I even get a say in this?" His tone is light, but I can sense a bit of hesitation.

"Of course you fucking do," Damon growls. "I just thought you should experience what this feels like. Trust me," he adds, giving Silas a serious look. "Please."

Silas sighs. "Yeah, sure. Be gentle with me, Brooks."

My thighs clench when he agrees. I walk to the bed and sit down, lying back as Silas walks over, grabbing my feet and spreading them wide.

"You have the most beautiful pussy," he mutters, his voice hoarse. "Pink, tight, glistening." He reaches down and rubs a few circles around my cunt, spreading the wetness. I see Damon lube up his shaft, coming to stand behind Silas. He reaches out a hand to caress Silas's neck, running it down the side of his arm next.

"Tell me if you want me to stop," he murmurs in Silas's ear. His gentle voice startles me. "Now fuck her." He looks at me. "Watch him as I fuck him, Lennon. Feel how hard he comes inside of you because of it."

Silas groans and pushes into me with zero warning, and I cry out as I adjust. "Oh, fuck," I whimper, feeling his hardness all the way into my stomach. My pussy is burning from the size of him, but then I get used to the fullness. He reaches down and places a hand around my throat. "Yes," I whisper. "Tighter." Silas's hand closes around the delicate flesh of my neck with more pressure. I see Damon grab Silas's hips.

"Ready, Silas?" Damon murmurs.

Silas lets out a primal sound, and he stills as Damon enters his ass.

"Oh fuck, oh fuck," Silas groans, his head bowing as Damon slowly pushes into him. I feel Silas's cock jump inside of me, turning into a steel rod as Damon moves in and out slowly. "This is..." he trails off, and I notice his hand is shaking around my neck. I run my hand up his arm. "I can already tell I'm going to explode inside of you," Silas growls, leaning down and pressing his lips to mine in a scorching kiss that has my clit throbbing. "I don't think you're ready, princess," he jokes as he pulls away, smirking.

And then he begins to fuck me, driving into me and then out fully, meeting Damon's cock at the same time. Just watching Silas experience this—the way his face is so open and vulnerable, and how he trembles slightly whenever Damon pounds into him—is more than enough to make me begin to buck my hips and meet Silas's thrusts. Silas begins to do circles on my clit with his fingers, and I arch my back. He removes his hand and I prop myself up on my elbows so that I can watch as Silas comes undone on top of me.

"Holy shit, Brooks," Silas chokes out. "Holy fucking shit."

"Come for me. Both of you," Damon commands. "Fill her up as I fill you, Silas. How does it feel to be fucked while fucking?"

Silas just roars in answer, slamming into me and gripping the flesh at my sides. His hips begin to undulate slowly, and I can tell by the way his cock curves upward that he's about to explode inside of me.

"That's fucking it, Huxley," Damon moans. "Your ass is gripping my cock. Do you know that?"

Silas bellows as his orgasm hits him, his face blazing.

"Oh fuck, I'm fucking coming so fucking hard," Silas rasps out, his voice uneven as he groans and shakes on top of me, his cock throbbing and stretching me as his forceful and violent orgasm rips through his body.

I throw my head back as my orgasm overtakes me quickly at the sight of him. My legs quake as my pussy grips onto Silas, contracting around his stiff shaft. I feel a gush of liquid rush out of me and onto Damon's bed just as Damon howls, spilling into Silas. We're all panting as the last of it leaves our bodies.

Silas looks dazed and confused, and his cock is still twitching inside of me.

Damon chuckles as he pulls out. "Well, that was really fucking fun."

"I lied. *That* was the hottest thing I've ever seen." I feel Damon's duvet. "I think I made a mess of your blanket, Damon."

He just walks over to his bathroom, grabbing us washcloths so we can all clean up.

"Don't worry about it, princess. I want nothing more than to fall asleep to the smell of your cunt, I can assure you."

I wrinkle my nose as we all take a quick shower together, smiling when I see Damon give Silas a covert high five.

By the time we're all dressed again and headed downstairs, I see a pair of headlights in the driveway. A few seconds later, Jude walks through the door and waves goodbye to who I can only presume is Liam.

When he closes and locks the door, he sighs, leaning against the heavy wood. He looks *exhausted*.

"So?" Silas asks, crossing his arms. "What happened?"

Jude shrugs, throwing his hands wide. He grins up at us. "You're looking at the newest member of the Church of the Rapture. I'm in. Liam believes me. Now it's time to do a little digging." He walks past us to his bedroom and then he stills, turning to face me. Quickly bending down, he gives me a slow kiss on the lips, lifting my chin with his finger and sniffing. "The next time you all decide to fuck, at least have the manners to wait for me."

thirteen

Damon

I follow Jude into his bedroom, shutting the door behind me. "So? Now what?"

Jude sighs and sits on his bed, running his hands over his face. "I'm not sure. He made me sign some confidentiality papers—just stupid shit like how I won't go to the press about anything I see, non-disclosures, things like that. He invited me to speak at the next service, just to introduce myself."

I let out a long, slow breath. "Fuck. Either he's playing us or he's a total idiot."

"It's the latter," he answers, leaning back on my elbows. "He thinks I'm a conflicted soul, anxious about the afterlife. You have to give me credit. I'm an amazing actor."

I chuckle, walking over to where he's sitting. "True."

My eyes find his, and his golden irises blaze into mine. "Did you have a nice evening?" he asks politely. I see right through the façade, grinning at his innuendo.

"It was... one for the books," I muse, taking another step toward him.

Jude's lips twitch. "I'm sure you'll all sleep very well tonight," he adds, smirking.

I nod, reaching down for Jude's hand. He stares at it for a few seconds, looking up at me with a darkened expression. He's always been the more hesitant one—always a bit unsure of himself when our relationship crosses a boundary. We go way back to before I even came out, but now I'm proud of my bisexuality. I love the guy, and though I could never date him because of his psychotic tendencies, I do have fun when we fuck. I wish he'd admit that he had fun, too.

"It's late," Jude says slowly. He's giving me an out, but I don't want one. I don't move my hand, and to my delight, Jude takes it.

Pulling him up, I barely register the bulge in his pants before his lips are on mine. The shock sends a heated wave through me, and I pull his head closer to mine as his tongue darts in and out of my mouth. I kiss him harder, groaning into his parted lips.

"Fuck you, Brooks," Jude murmurs, and I can feel his smile.

"Go right ahead," I retort before his lips are back on mine, nipping and sucking in a frenzy.

Our hips crash against each other's, and I grind myself against him. My hands fist his shirt and pull him closer, moaning when I feel him thrust into me—his hard cock rubbing mine through our pants.

I pull away from his lips with a groan, reaching down and unbuttoning his pants. He watches me with darkened eyes. The only sound is our heavy breathing. I smile up at him and cup his erection, and the sound that rumbles through him is low and throaty, sending a tingle straight to my groin. I pull his boxers down to free his cock, and he hisses as I stroke it.

"Fuck," he murmurs, his voice ragged. I drop down to my knees and Jude's hands automatically grip the back of my hair. I have to give him credit—he's a total alpha in the bedroom, and I fucking love relinquishing control to him. There's a certain sort of thrill letting Jude Vanderbilt have his way with you.

I take his cock fully into my mouth, and he inhales sharply, holding me with his cock in the back of my mouth. One of his hands comes to my throat.

"I want to feel you swallow me whole."

Fuck.

Despite just coming in Silas, I reach down and unbutton my pants, gripping my heavy shaft and stroking it quickly.

Jude moans every time I move him in and out of my mouth. When he pulls out, I glance up at him, using my tongue to flick the tip of his dick. He watches me intently, tugging his lower lip between his teeth, his brows furrowed as he tries to fuck my mouth.

"Did I tell you to stop?" he asks cruelly. His grip on my throat tightens.

I work my cock in my hand, feeling my orgasm building as Jude takes control. Opening my mouth, I let him fuck it exactly how he wants, while my hips thrust into my hand, my erection stiffening and curving upward. I take his cock out of my mouth.

"Fuck, you're making me come," I rasp.

"I want to come with you," he groans, letting go of my throat.

I release the hold on my throbbing cock, letting out a

feral cry. I was *two seconds away* from spilling all over his floor, and it's heavy and aching, ready for release.

Jude helps me up and kisses me fiercely, grabbing my head and pressing his hips into me. His length is still wet from my mouth, and we fuck each other, our cocks sliding up and down along one another's frantically. Moaning into his mouth, I grab his ass and hold him in place, grinding my hips with more purpose, my swollen cock against his, which feels hard as steel.

"Oh fuck, oh fuck," Jude says quietly, his voice frayed. A red-hot jolt shoots through me at his desperate words.

And then I feel him stiffen against me.

I up my tempo, grunting with every thrust as I chase my release, feeling myself yell loudly as the first of Jude's hot come spills onto my cock. I use it as lube, feeling my balls tighten and my own cock harden. It pulses against his wet cock, shooting large ropes of come all over his stomach. When we're finished, I just pull him closer, hugging him as we catch our breath.

"Holy shit," I whisper, my chest still heaving.

"That was fun and unexpected," he answers. And then he kisses me. "Thank you. I know why you did it."

I smirk, pulling away and walking into his bathroom to get us towels to clean ourselves up.

"Now you'll sleep well, too."

fourteen

Lennon

I park and walk into Lola's condo complex, trying not to blush when I pass the same stairwell where Silas and I had sex. I go up to the third floor, smiling when Lola opens her door, throwing her arms around me.

"Okay, how much candy do I need to ply you with to convince you to run this bakery with me?" she asks right off the bat.

I step inside, admiring her style. The walls are white, and the furniture is minimalist with cooler tones and pops of color. There are hundreds of books organized by color in a massive bookshelf, a standout dark green couch, bright green accents everywhere to coordinate, and when I look into the kitchen, I can see that the cupboards and counters are black.

In a nutshell, this condo is one-hundred percent Lola.

"Hi, and by the way, I love your place," I say, bypassing her question, running my fingers over the spines of all the

SAVAGE GODS

old books. "It doesn't even look like you have a kid," I muse, taking in the pristine living area. I don't even see a rogue toy.

"Thanks. Isaiah is kind of a neat freak, and Remi has her very own playroom for all her ugly as sin toys," she jokes.

"Remi?" I ask, realizing I never knew her daughter's name. "That's a cute name."

Lola smiles, running a hand through her long, dark hair. "Thanks." She clasps her hands together. "So, about that candy..."

I laugh. "I don't want to disappoint you if I say no," I answer, sitting down on her couch. She jogs into the kitchen and comes back with a bowl of mini candy bars. When I lift my eyebrows, she shakes her head and sits down next to me.

"Isaiah has a sweet tooth, what can I say? It's like Willy Wonka in here most days. He gave up drugs and alcohol, but now he's a sugar fiend."

I giggle and take a chocolate bar. "Here's the thing..." I pause, taking a bite. "I want to do this. Owning a bakery with you sounds amazing. But full disclosure: I have zero money to my name, and I also don't know if I want to settle down in Greythorn, you know?"

She nods, her expression serious. "Yeah. I feel that. But let me ask you a question, if I may."

I finish my chocolate and grab another one. "Go right ahead."

"Okay. You and the guys... you're..." she trails off, making a vulgar gesture with her hands. "Am I right?"

I nod sheepishly with a small chuckle. "Yep."

She grins, shaking her head. "On the one hand, they're like brothers to me, but on the other hand..." She blows out a breath of air. "I mean, how did it happen?" I open my mouth to explain, but she cuts me off. "Wait, wait, wait. Let me finish my spiel."

I smile, leaning back against the buttery leather as I chew my chocolate. "Continue your spiel."

She sits up straighter and turns to face me. "Okay, you and the guys are an item. And they've made their lives here, despite not loving every second of it. And yes, you may all go back to Boston one day and live happily ever after. But realistically? You're going to fall in love, maybe pop out a baby or two, and voila, five years have passed, and you've got nothing to show for it." I go to retort, but she continues. "Take a page from their book. If you open a shop here, with yours truly, maybe it will do well enough for us to open a sister bakery in Boston in the future." She wiggles her eyebrows, and I sag against the back of the couch.

"Man, you're good."

She smirks. "Is that a yes?"

I twist my lips to the side. Running a bakery with Lola *would* be my dream. Something about her spiel gives me the good kind of nervous butterflies again, and I realize it was her comment about popping out babies. Why am I suddenly so eager to reproduce? Is this what people call the biological clock ticking? I blame Ledger and Briar, and their stupid baby.

"It's a *maybe*," I answer. "Leaning toward yes, but not quite ready to sign a contract."

Lola squeals. "That's okay! Oh my God, this is the best news. We need to come up with a name."

I roll my eyes. "Let me process what I've just *maybe* agreed to, please."

Her eyes go big and watery, and she takes my hand. "In all seriousness, I've never really had a woman friend." She swallows. "They're always put off by the tattoos and piercings, and the hair, and the clothes..." she trails off, and my eyes rove over her black, flowy dress.

"I love your style," I add, smiling as I squeeze her hands.

"My point is, I'm really fucking grateful you walked into Savage Ink all those weeks ago. Because this is nice. And I really like you."

My chest begins to ache, and I tamp down the feeling of wanting to make a joke or wanting to push her away. Instead, I squeeze her hands again.

"Me too."

She hands me another candy bar. "Okay. Now that I have a tentative yes from my future business partner, I need *all the deets* about how you came to be fucking Silas, Damon, and Jude at the same time." I let out a loud laugh, but Lola holds up a finger. "And don't leave a single detail out."

fifteen

Lennon

I tug the cami over my head, tossing it onto the bed and groaning in frustration. *Why does getting dressed for a date seem so daunting?* I walk back to the closet and pick out a simple, black lace dress that fits like a second skin. Standing in front of the mirror, I adjust the length of the skirt so it covers my ass, and then I slip into heeled black booties and a denim jacket. I pull my hair around over my shoulders, fluffing it out a bit and biting my lower lip as I assess my reflection.

One, it's Sunday, and Jude is taking me on a date in Boston. A *fancy* date. Two, Jude is a romantic, because instead of staying behind during one of the infamous parties, he's taking me out alone. A small part of me trills with excitement, because I truly have no idea what's to come–no pun intended. He's so unpredictable. The opposite of Wright and my old life. Smiling, I swipe on some nude lipstick, and as I pull the door open, Jude has his hand raised, ready to knock.

The bad thing about going on a date with your roommate is that one second, you're choosing your outfit, and the next second, your date is picking you up at the door of your room. There's no time to decompress or mentally prepare–no last glance at your reflection in the bathroom mirror.

Oh well.

"Wow," he remarks, his voice rough as his eyes appraise me. "You look..." he trails off, taking a step back and drinking me in unabashedly. "Simply edible."

I smile, taking in his crisp white shirt, with a couple of the top buttons undone, and dark grey slacks. His sleeves are rolled up a few times, showing off his arms. *Whoa*. Jude Vanderbilt in a shirt and slacks is... unnerving. He looks so normal. If I saw him walking down the street, he'd blend in with every other late-twenties man on his way home from work–minus the dazzling copper eyes, twisted smirk, and corded forearms. Even as a normal guy, he'd still catch my attention any day of the week.

"You look amazing too," I tell him, my voice all breathy. He pulls out a single black rose from behind his back, and I gasp. "This is beautiful." I touch the velvety skin of the flower.

"It reminded me of you. If you were a rose, Lennon Rose, you'd be thorny and black–stubborn, yet unique. Classic. Moody."

My knees buckle, and I look up into his eyes. "Thank you." I twist around and walk to my dresser, sticking it in the glass of water I brought up earlier. My hands tremble slightly when I wipe them on my dress, heading back to where Jude is standing.

"Shall we?" he asks, his voice smooth. He holds a hand out for me, and my stomach flips when our hands meet.

I don't say anything as he leads me out to his car, the other guys nowhere to be seen.

After a thirty-minute commute into Boston, Jude manages to find parking in a multi-level garage in the north end. We talk about Savage Ink, he updates me on Liam and Church of the Rapture, much to my chagrin, and then we get onto the subject of high school, and all the embarrassing things we did when we were kids. As he pulls into the industrial garage, my stomach dips again.

These men—this life with them—it's *fun*. And I'm really starting to like all of them in their own ways. I would've never expected this from Jude, but that fact alone has me grinning as he holds my door open for me, pulling me into him, and planting a soft kiss on my lips.

Jude-who-fucks-me-with-a-cross is great, but romantic-date-night-Jude takes the cake. I never would've guessed.

He leads me through a maze of historic buildings, all with red brick, ivy, and vintage signs, to the waterfront—the Charles River nearly lapping at our feet. I sigh, breathing in the mossy scent of the river. It feels and smells like home here.

"I miss it, too," Jude says from next to me, leaning against the railing and turning to face me. "Every fucking day."

"Will you guys ever move back?" I ask, a little nervous as I wait for his answer.

He nods. "I think so. We all love it too much to leave it

forever. But until all this shit with the church is done..."

"I know," I acquiesce. "One day."

"Hungry?" he asks, leading me to the fancy-looking place hovering over the river. I see glasses and multiple sets of plates at each table setting, and silver napkin holders that nearly blind me from here. My mouth fills with saliva. I made the mistake of attempting to work out with the guys today, and I gravely underestimated how hard exercising is, and how hungry it would make me. I can barely lift my arms as we go through the revolving glass doors. Jude holds me close as the host walks us to a secluded area in the back, away from the rest of the people. I look around and lift an eyebrow.

"Oh, someone's trying to get laid later tonight," I tease, sitting down in the chair he pulls out for me. There is a candle with wax dripping over an old wine bottle, and as the host gets us settled in our seats, Jude sets a little black bag on the pristine white tablecloth. Then he props his hands up on the table.

"Are you sure you want to wait until later?"

I cock my head. "What is that?" I reach out for it, but he picks it up and holds it just out of reach.

"You're going to excuse yourself to the restroom," he commands, his voice low. "And you're going to wear this."

My eyes widen and whole body heats at his words, my clit pulsing as I stare at the mysterious bag.

I change my mind. I fucking *love* romantic-slash-sex-God-Jude.

Fucking.

Love.

I stand up and clear my throat, and Jude hands the black bag to me. I tuck it into the pocket of my jacket and excuse myself. Trying to keep my knees from trembling, I make it to the marble-laden ladies' room, and there are several older women reapplying their lipstick in the wall-sized, gilded mirror. I give them a small smile before disappearing into a stall, trying not to fumble with whatever the fuck Jude has up his sleeve. When I pull it out, I laugh loudly, and someone clears their throat.

I don't know what I expected–perhaps a pair of hot pink underwear, or some sort of lingerie.

Instead, a large, curved vibrator lands in my hands, and I stare at it for a second too long before grinning.

I have *no* idea how this is supposed to go in, but after holding it out and studying it, there's only one way it can go. It's like a U, with a small bit on one side, and an egg-shaped bit on the other side. I prop a leg up and insert the egg into myself, letting the smaller side rest comfortably against my clit. I didn't see an on button, but of course, Jude is probably the one who will be controlling that.

I exit the stall and wash my hands, and one of the ladies eyes me suspiciously, her pearls hanging around her neck like a noose.

Like my mother.

Walking back to the table, I remove my jacket and hand Jude the black bag.

"Keep it," he says indifferently, leaning back with a smug smile. "You're going to need something to hold your wet panties." Leaning forward, he reaches out for my hand. "Until I can lap it all up." I open and close my mouth, anticipatory excitement rolling through me.

Nothing should shock me with Jude, yet here we are.

I lean back and pretend he didn't just make my night a thousand times better. Instead, I sip my water, looking anywhere but at his face.

"Lennon," he says slowly. I pretend not to hear him,

smiling up at the server when he asks us what type of water we want and answering quickly. "Lennon," he says again, his deeper tone causing a shiver to roll through me as I hum once in acknowledgement.

Before he can say my name again, the vibrator shocks me, making me jump and grip the edge of the table as I glare at him, my face, neck, and chest flushed with heat.

Holy.

Fuck.

My pussy instantly clenches around the vibrating egg, and I can feel my own wetness getting buzzed around my clit as the intensity grows. I look down at Jude's hands, and he's holding a small remote that could pass as a fancy car fob.

Son of a bitch.

"Next time you decide not to answer me, I'll turn it all the way up to ten."

I inhale sharply, my nails digging into the table. "What level is it at now?" I hate the way my voice sounds desperate and faint. He *knows* what he does to me.

"One," he answers, his eyebrows knitting together as his lips twist to the side. I see him click a button again, and the intensity doubles. "Two."

"Holyyyy fuuuuck," I whisper, unconsciously rocking my hips in the chair. *Gods, this feels fucking amazing.* I feel my whole lower half coil up, and I open my mouth.

It's not possible I could come so soon, is it? There's no w–

Another click, and I throw my head back, holding back the moan in my throat as my whole body begins to tremble. I can feel myself milking the vibrator, as the orgasm slowly begins to crest with one sweet, glorious pulse after the other. It's purely physical. The vibrator is positioned against both sensitive areas, and I know my body is going to react whether I want it to or not.

So close, I am so close–

The vibrating stops, and Jude shifts to tuck the remote in his pants pocket as I pant across from him. I feel a drop of sweat run down my back, and when I let go of the table, my hands are cramped from gripping it so tightly.

I'm about to yell at him when the server comes back over with our waters. I take mine and gulp it all down, and Jude just smiles up at him.

"She's had a long day. Could I please get a bottle of the 2012 Dom Perignon?"

"Of course, Mr. Vanderbilt." He walks away, and I stare at Jude in shock.

"He knows your name."

"I used to come here all the time," he says, smirking. "On dates."

My frown deepens. "You're a pig."

Before I can process what's happening, the vibrator starts up again, and I nearly levitate out of my seat.

"Oh my *God*," I whisper.

Clutching the table again, I feel my whole body clench around the vibrator, and just then, the server walks back over with the champagne, and Jude nonchalantly clicks the vibrator up a notch. I whimper, and the server looks down at me.

"Are you alright, Mrs. Vanderbilt?" he asks, and I have to actively try not to cry out. He called me *Mrs. Vanderbilt–*

My pussy flutters around the hard egg inside of me.

"I—um—I'm fine," I mutter, looking anywhere but at Jude's face. I sincerely hope no one can see the light sheen of sweat on my forehead, or the way I'm sure my chest is all blotchy.

The server nods. "Very well. Who is approving the champagne?" he asks, holding the bottle over the table.

"She is," Jude says, his voice light and tinged with amusement.

Prick.

The server slowly—so agonizingly slowly—pops the champagne cork off noiselessly, setting it down next to the stainless-steel bucket of ice. He pours me a bit of champagne, and as I pick it up, biting my lower lip until it's nearly bleeding, Jude ramps up the vibrations one more time.

I've lost track of what number this is—but I know from the way my core is gripping the egg, and the way I can feel how wet my underwear is already, that this orgasm is going to be explosive, and it's going to happen whether the server is here or not—and whether I want it to happen or not.

I squeeze my legs together, but it only intensifies the feelings. Gasping, I spread my legs and arch my back slightly.

It's too hot in here. Waves of pleasure shoot down every limb. My body is beginning to betray me.

I take a quick sip, nodding once. "Yep. Great. Thank you."

Jude makes a disapproving sound. "Come on, honey. Give me another taste before we decide."

Click.

I let out a string of hushed swear words, and the server's eyebrows knit together in concern.

"Are you sure you're okay?" he asks, placing a hand on my shoulder.

Oh. God.

I pick the glass up, panting as my orgasm rips through me, not caring that some other man's hand is on my shoulder, not caring that I'm about to have the most explosive orgasm of my life. I bring the glass to my lips and close my eyes as my body undulates against the vibrator, wave upon wave tearing through me quickly, a fiery blaze making me cry out, quaking in my seat as my hips move without permission. The part vibrating against my clit starts to make a subtle, wet sound, and to my horror, I realize my lap is soaked, and it's beginning to run down my legs.

I swear and buck and hold the glass out as the server takes it, setting it down.

"Is she alright?" he asks, looking thoroughly concerned, tilting his head.

I am gasping for air, glaring at Jude, when he has the audacity to laugh. "She just really, really likes champagne."

sixteen

Lennon

After a delicious dinner–and after I forgive him for humiliating me–Jude takes me on a tour of his favorite parts of the north end of Boston.

Minus the vibrator, which is now stored back in its bag.

We walk past his favorite bakery, his favorite Italian place, and then as we round the corner, I stop in my tracks as I take in the sign above a tattoo shop.

"Is this–"

Jude puts an arm around my shoulders and guides me into Ignite Ink–the sister shop of Savage Ink.

It's different in a lot of ways, yet oddly familiar. There are large, gilded frames like in Savage, but instead of damask wallpaper, the wallpaper here is dark green. The couch is a faded black leather, and the wood floor has been laid in a herringbone pattern. There are several people hovering over clients, and a receptionist clicking away on the computer. He cranes his neck over the screen and grins when he sees us.

"Oh my God," he says, standing. He's tall and thin, with short black hair and a septum piercing. He doesn't have any visible tattoos, and he's wearing platform Doc Martens. I instantly know I'm going to like him. "Did the infamous Jude Vanderbilt decide to bless us with his presence?" He pretends to fan himself. "How lucky we are." He walks over and pulls Jude into a tight hug, then turns to me, smiling.

"I'm Levi. I run this shithole."

I laugh. "Lennon."

"Ooh, cool name. Named after John Lennon?"

I shake my head. "I wish. My parents weren't that cool." My eyes flick to Jude, and his eyes burn into mine as we both remember how pissed off he was when my mom showed up a few weeks ago.

"Let's get you a tour, missy."

I drag my eyes away from Jude's as Levi shows me around, and I meet the tattoo artists that Silas, Damon, and Jude all trained. Even though they don't work here anymore, I can see traces of them everywhere, with their designs hanging on the walls. Levi gets Jude and me a beer and we all chat on the couch until a large group of clients show up, and Jude and I duck out of Ignite.

As we walk back out to the street, Jude takes my hand in his.

"Do you miss it?"

He knows what I'm asking. "I do." Stopping at the river, he turns to me. The air is warm and humid—we both took our jackets off during our walk. "But it's not mine anymore. If we moved back, I think we'd try doing something different." He smiles down at me. "I quite like Savage Ink. We have this hot new assistant and everything."

I punch his arm, and he chuckles as we head back to the car.

Once inside, Jude turns to face me. "Come here." His voice is less rough, more fragmented and vulnerable. I crawl over the center console, straddling his lap. "You are unraveling me, Lennon Rose," he growls, his words sinking in and wrapping around my heart as his hands grip my hips possessively.

"Likewise," I whisper, breathing him in. I reach out and brush a piece of light brown hair from his forehead, and his hooded, golden eyes flutter ever so slightly. "I need you to promise me that you're going to be careful. With Liam, with the church…" I trail off, suddenly wanting to hug him and never let go.

"I promise," he says, pulling my lips to his with one hand fisting my hair, and the other grabbing the flesh on my waist, shimmying my dress up.

He groans into my mouth, his tongue swirling with mine, as he unzips his pants and moves my underwear to the side. The movements of both his lips and his hands are fervent and frantic. He's tearing at himself like he can't move quick enough, tugging at my lips like he only wants to breathe my air.

"I wish I could've lapped you up earlier, in the restaurant," Jude growls. I feel the warm head of his cock tease my entrance.

"Me too," I answer, breathlessly, feeling just as desperate for him as he is for me.

"Your little pussy is so eager," he teases, and then he drives into me, thrusting his hips upward. I cry out as he fills me to the hilt, stretching me. His piercings barrel through me, and I feel myself grip onto him.

"Can you blame me?" I ask on the end of a moan, moving my hips on top of him. "You're such a prick."

Jude smirks. "You liked it, princess."

"I like you," I admit, my voice hardly a whisper. He thrusts into me in response, and I concede. "And yes. I fucking loved it."

His head dips to kiss my neck as he concentrates on properly fucking me, and I reach up, grabbing the handle for support.

"Ride me," he orders, his voice frayed.

So I do. I move my hips on top of him, sliding upwards just enough to get us the much-needed friction. Circling my hips, I can tell by the way his copper eyes are nearly black, and the way he has his lower lip between his teeth, that he's close. That fact alone makes me ride him faster, harder. The sound of my arousal, mixed with the slapping of our skin, makes me cry out. The piercings on his cock massage my insides, creating a deep, intense feeling of needing to release—a gnawing, tingling ache that goes all the way to my fingers and toes. His ladder piercing provides a whole-body experience.

I feel my pussy begin to ripple around him, and the primal noise that comes out of his throat sends me over the edge.

"Oh fuck, princess," he groans, suddenly taking my hips and fucking me hard and fast from beneath. "I can feel you coming on my cock," he adds, slamming into me.

I close my eyes and explode, feeling myself release completely, the sweet, all-consuming euphoria ripping through every muscle, every nerve.

"Fuck, fuck, fuck," Jude rasps, his voice filled with pure need. "You're soaking me." He grips me harder. "I'm going to come."

I open my eyes and watch as he fills me with his come, as his cock bobs inside of me, still firmly gripped by my pussy. I feel him–the pulses of pleasure. He empties himself inside of me and then slips out slowly as we pant together. I collapse against his body.

His hands work their way along my ass, rubbing me softly, caressing me gently. Both hands come up my body to my arms, and then they grip my hair and pull me away from him so he can look me in the eyes.

"I think I fucking love you, Lennon Rose," Jude says with his gaze locked onto mine, his voice softer than I've ever heard it.

I swallow thickly, suddenly emotional. I'd be lying if I said I didn't feel the same way–didn't share some sort of strange bond with Jude Vanderbilt. From the day he told my mother off and punched a mirror all those weeks ago... something happened that night. And we'd been falling, uncontrollably, ever since.

"I think I love you, too," I whisper, bending down and kissing him until we're both breathless once again.

seventeen

Lennon

I wring my hands as I wait for Briar at Romancing the Bean. I'm early, which isn't completely out of the norm. But I am nervous to officially sit and chat with her. I'm not sure why, either. I think it's because she's evidence that this isn't just a game we're all playing. Polyamory is real, and she's living proof. I'm not in a fever dream. This is real life.

I love hanging out with the guys. They each bring something different to the table. But as someone who has only ever had two men in her life–and both ended up being jerks–this is all new territory for me. I can't deny the love that's beginning to form with each of them–and between all of us at the same time–but I haven't let myself think of what all of this means, until now.

I see Briar walk through the front door, and I hold up a hand to signal her over. She smiles and saunters toward me, Easton nowhere to be found. I'm slightly disappointed by that fact, which is disconcerting as someone who never even entertained the idea of children until the last few weeks.

"Hey," Briar says, sitting down and sighing. "Sorry I'm late."

I shake my head. "I was early. I think you're right on time."

She chuckles and leans forward. She's dressed in a casual white dress. Her auburn hair is down and flowing, and she has on minimal makeup. "That's a damn miracle with a five-month-old."

I huff a laugh. "Has it been hard?" I ask casually, handing her the plate of assorted muffins that I ordered when I arrived.

She nods, grabbing one. "Besides my partners, I think you're the first person to ask me that." She sighs, and I feel a pang of empathy in my chest. "It's been... *really* hard. I mean, of course, right? Having a baby is hard for everyone." She takes a bite of the muffin. "The guys are a huge help, though. Samson, my partner, has him right now. But between pumping and sleeping and making baby food... I have like zero time to myself." She sighs. "I'm not complaining about his fathers, either. They show up, they do the work. But it's just so heavy and daunting, being a parent." Her voice gets quiet. "I don't know if I'm cut out for it." I don't want to interrupt her because she seems like she needs to vent, so I take a massive bite of my muffin. I wonder if she has female friends she can talk to about this?

"And my mom, God..." she trails off. "She's like the most natural mother ever." I laugh, and Briar quirks an eyebrow. "I'm serious. She's wonder woman. So I sort of feel like I'm failing compared to her."

I nod, digesting all this information, but before I can respond, she groans.

"I'm sorry. I totally just dumped all of that on you and we barely know each other."

I smile. "It's okay. It seems like you needed to get it out. And I'm here to listen." I tilt my head as I play with the crumbs of the muffin I just scarfed. "Besides, there may come a day where I need to vent to you about parenthood."

Briar's face softens, and her eyes make their way to my stomach. "Oh my God, are you–"

I shake my head vehemently. "God, no. Not yet. Not for a little while. IUD is firmly lodged in there, if you know what I mean?"

She nods. "Okay. For a second, I thought you were telling me that you're pregnant. And I got excited, because we're kind of like sisters now."

My chest aches at her words, and something warm rushes through me.

Sisters.

I always wanted a sister growing up, always wanted someone to commiserate with about my parents. And I realize, as I look at her, that we're going to be good friends. *The best.* It's different than it was with Lola. With Briar, something connects when she looks at me, and I feel like I can tell her anything. She's open without being obvious about it, and I appreciate that. I know I can trust her instantly. My soul recognizes something in her.

I look up at Briar and take her hand. "Why does it feel like we've known each other forever?" I ask.

She squeezes my hand. "Right? I thought it was just me. Maybe because we're brother fuckers."

I spit out my muffin, much to the chagrin of the neighboring table. The elderly woman glares at us as we both descend into a fit of giggles. The server brings us our drinks.

"Okay, but seriously," she gasps, grinning. "I want to hear how this all happened."

I shake my head. "No way. You go first."

She smirks, stirring sugar into her latte that the server just dropped off. "Fine. I met them my senior year at Ravenwood Academy," she tells me slowly. I do the math in my head. Her and Ledger are four years younger than us, so she was there after me. "Hunter, one of my partners, ended up being the son of the man my mom married–"

I hold my hand out, my mouth open. "Hold up. One of your partners is your stepbrother?"

She wrinkles her nose. "Technically, yes."

I laugh. "No judgment here. Go on."

"Well, as you probably know, I got to know him and his best friends a little too well... they were bullies at first, but like not really, you know? They were just confused because I was the first person to defy them."

I smile. "I know that feeling."

She laughs. "I went to college in Paris, and we kept our poly relationship going. And then when the time came to try for Easton, we decided we didn't want to know who the father was. Because they were all his father."

"That's sweet," I answer, looking down at my tea. If–*if* I ever decided to have children with the guys, would I want to do the same thing?

"He was born nine months later," she continues, rolling her eyes. "They'll never let me live that down. They were so proud of impregnating me on the first try."

I snort. "Sounds about right."

"We lived together for a while in a small house, but when Easton was born, I begged them for my own place." She pauses. "Some poly couples live together, but I needed–no, I *need*–my own place." She says this resolutely, and I wonder, as I study the dark bags under her eyes, if I should offer to watch him or help out somehow? "When Easton is with one of them, I need that alone time. So now I have my own house, and Easton splits his time with all of us, but always comes to me at night because he's still nursing. I'm sure we'll re-evaluate that when I wean him, but for now, it works. Most days, we all end up there for dinner and to put him to bed, but I have the option of being alone, too."

"Sounds like the dream," I joke, and she laughs again. "What do you do for work?"

She takes another bite of a muffin. "I'm a therapist." Wiping her face off, she shrugs. "You probably wouldn't guess that from my one-sided rant when I walked in, though."

"No, I think it makes total sense," I add, smirking.

"Really?"

I nod. "You came in here and you were comfortable expressing yourself to me. Totally and completely. I could use some help with that." I bite the inside of my cheek. "I didn't have the best childhood, so I tend to bottle it all up inside until it explodes. I had a therapist in New York, but I obviously don't see her anymore."

She gives me a sympathetic smile. "I can refer you to one of my colleagues if you want?"

I nod, swallowing down the thickness in my throat. "That would be wonderful. Thank you." I look down at my hands, feeling suddenly emotional. "I clam up when I'm nervous, or when I feel anything, really. It's hard for me to accept the fact that people love me. It took me almost five years of therapy to begin to love myself, because no one loved me when I was growing up."

She blows a loud breath of air out. "That's rough. If

your parents aren't there to teach you what love looks like, it's so hard to learn as an adult."

I nod once. "Yeah, you can say that again."

"But it's not impossible," she adds optimistically, giving me a kind smile. My heart cracks just a bit at the expression on her face.

Yep. Fast friends. I can feel it already.

"It sounds like you're doing the work," she offers, using a voice I can only assume is the one she saves for her clients. "Which is a start."

"True."

She grabs her phone. "I'm going to put a reminder in my phone. I'll shoot you a text later with Gia's number. She's great." Setting her phone down, she grabs her coffee, leans back in her chair, and clears her throat. "So, what's your story, Lennon Rose?"

I scoff. "Did Silas tell you my full name?"

She gives me a goofy smile. "No. But by the time I got to Ravenwood Academy, you were like a legend."

My cheeks heat. "God, you must think I'm a horrible person."

"Nuh-uh, stop that," she commands, shaking her head. "You forget I fell in love with the Kings of Ravenwood Academy. They were bullies, too. I'm no stranger to the deeper reasons someone resorts to bullying."

Her words pin me to the spot. Does her job make her more perceptive or something?

"Well, my parents had me and basically decided when I was about six that they didn't want to be parents anymore. They started leaving me home with the nanny all the time and essentially neglecting me. Because they weren't parenting me, I was an emotional wreck. You can imagine what that does to a hormonal teenager."

Briar nods, her brows furrowed. "That sounds like it was really hard."

I swallow, nodding. "It was. So I left–moved to Cambridge and went to Harvard. I met Wright, my ex, and we moved to Manhattan after school. I thought I loved him, but him cheating on me ended up being the best thing that ever happened to me. So, fast forward to two months ago, and boom. I ended up back here, in the apartment above Savage Ink. I bet you can guess what happened next."

She smiles and stirs her coffee. "Those baby blues got you too, huh?"

I cock my head. "Baby blues?"

She laughs. "The Huxley eyes."

I chuckle. "Oh, yeah." Taking a sip of tea, I think back to that first night–the night Silas told me to fuck off.

She leans forward conspiratorially. "Have you had sex in the chapel yet?"

I nearly spit out my drink. "What? Have *you*?"

She shrugs. "Let's just say it's a religious experience." Taking my hand again, she smiles softly. "I'm glad Silas found you. He's... happier than I've ever seen him. So are the other guys." She pauses, looking down for a second. "And it's nice to have someone to talk to about this. Because sometimes things get weird. Like when people ask which one I'm legally married to." I snort, but I'm curious, too. She must see it on my face. "The answer is none of them. Marriage is confined to outdated laws and traditions. I feel like as a group of people in a polyamorous relationship, we're well past all that."

"Not in Utah," I quip, and she cackles.

"But seriously, if you have any questions about the logistics, or questions that should be simple, like what size bed to get... just ask me. I've been with my partners for six years. We've seen it all."

The warm feeling returns, and I don't say anything as the server takes our empty mugs and sets another plate of muffins down. Briar just looks at me with that goofy smile again, and there it is–that feeling of being accepted. Of feeling like you've found a true friend, the kind some people only have on TV shows and in books. I don't know if it's because she's partnered with Silas's brother, or if it's because she seems like she's been through some shit, like me... but I'm eternally grateful to have found her.

eighteen

Jude

My foot taps against the pew in front of me as I watch Liam give his sermon. I've relocated to the front row now, making sure he sees me with a mildly interested expression. Anything to convince him that every fucking second in this church–if you can even call it that–doesn't repulse me. It's all going to be worth it. It's all going to work out. Liam is beginning to trust me, and I've made my hesitation believable. Now, it's just a matter of figuring out where they store their most prized possessions. Where they hide the dirt that can bring this whole fucking façade crumbling down.

I wring my hands in front of me as Liam speaks about sin. *The irony.* The Church of the Rapture is corrupt from the inside out. Pedophilia, human trafficking, drugs... the list goes on. They are small but powerful, with a lot of wealthy people who write them checks every single week. I have to figure out their weaknesses and expose them. I know they exist. It's what Oliver died trying to uncover.

But first, I have to get Liam to trust me wholly.

The sermon ends, and we all sing a few songs. It's such a crock of shit, and I hate every word that comes out of my mouth. Finally, the service is over, and Liam meets my gaze, gesturing for me to follow him.

We make our way down the hallway to what I assume is his office. It's generic and boring, clearly a front for something much more sinister. *All* of this seems like a front, to be honest. Even Liam. I watch him as he moves behind the desk, falling into his chair and sighing. Does anyone else know he prefers men? Does anyone really know him at all? Are they all hiding secrets? A shiver works down my spine when I think of what other people must be hiding. Greythorn has always had dark secrets of its own, and Church of the Rapture just plays into that.

These people are ruthless, their influence uncanny, and here I am, throwing myself right into the fighting pit.

"What'd you think?" Liam asks me with a studying stare, leaning back in his leather executive chair.

I don't answer at first, instead opting to pace around his office and pretend to look at his religious paraphernalia. There's a large cross behind him, and above it, a poster that says, *Live, Pray, Hope*. I train my mouth into a frown, disguising my amusement.

"It was interesting," I answer slowly, turning to face him. "Look, I'm not a saint. I've done some shit, you know?"

Liam chuckles. "As long as you are one of us, the Lord will forgive."

I bite the inside of my cheek. I know why Silas and Damon tasked me with this–why they asked me to go undercover. Silas couldn't, because Liam would never believe him. And Damon can't hide his feelings to save his life. He would've blown his cover during the first service.

But me?

I smile at Liam, narrowing my eyes. "It seems a little too good to be true. There has to be some sort of dark side to the church," I push, cocking my head. "Or are you all just really, really *good* people?" Liam's eyes bore into mine, but I continue. I must make this believable. "It's hard to take you all seriously because you all seem too perfect, like you have your shit together, you know?"

Liam's jaw ticks. *Fuck.* Maybe I pushed too hard, too soon.

"You know as well as I do that we're not perfect," Liam growls, leaning forward. "I know you'd be lying if you told me you didn't know what happened between Silas and I."

There it is.

I nod slowly. "Yes. He said you kissed him–"

Liam slams his fist against the wooden desk, effectively shutting me up. "A man lying with another man is a sin, Jude. Silas kissed me. He came onto *me*," he hisses.

I place my palms together, resting my chin on my fingers. "I see." I shrug. "Sorry. I didn't mean to insinuate anything."

Liam's eyes stay on my face for a second too long. My blood cools. He's a creepy ass dude. A predator. I know Silas is one of many that he's taken advantage of.

"We're not perfect," Liam adds, his voice softer now. "But we don't have to be. We're doing the Lord's work. Sometimes that doesn't compute with our earthly neighbors, and they call us a cult–freaks, weirdos, psychos. But we all know we're on the right side of things, and when the Lord calls us back up, we will leave this sinful wasteland."

Fuck.

He's completely insane.

I nod again, looking down at the floor. "I believe you, by

the way. I believe he'll call us back up. I am just trying to understand my place in all of this, because I know my past is questionable."

I look up, and Liam watches me for a beat. "We all start somewhere, Jude."

I furrow my brows in faux concern. "How do I get to a place where I can…" I trail off, running a hand through my hair.

Liam leans forward again. "Jude, if you're serious about growing your relationship with God, why don't you join our leadership meeting tomorrow?"

Bingo.

I shake my head. "I would feel like an imposter."

Liam stands, slapping me on the back. "Nonsense. You've proven yourself to me, showing up to every single service without missing a beat. Asking questions. Attempting to learn, attempting to grow." He pauses, smiling. "Now we just have to convince everyone else."

nineteen

Lennon

I walk through the bakery with Lola, my heart clenching with every passing second. *Of course* it's perfect–quaint, small enough to be intimate, with historical features such as high ceilings and crown molding leftover from another era. The floors are covered in black and white penny tiles, the kitchen is updated and clean, and the awning out front is a soft pink. I can already visualize everything–the logo, the glass cases full of our baked goods, and the fact that I'm a five-minute walk from Savage Ink...

I place both hands over my face and shake my head. "I fucking love it," I tell Lola, who has been waiting on bated breath.

She jumps up and down, squealing like a child, which must be a feat in her large platform sneakers.

"Oh my God, right? It's so cute." She puts an arm around me. "Look, I'm doing this whether or not you're by my side. If it'll make you feel better, why don't you help me out for a couple of months? I'll pay you, and we can see if we'd even like working together? If you like me enough after your trial period, I can officially put you on the lease.

I nod slowly. "Okay. Yes." I slap my forehead. "We're really doing this, aren't we?"

She squeals again, pulling me into a tight hug. "We just have to come up with a name now," she adds excitedly. Locking up, she walks me to my car. "Lennon's Lickable Treats," she suggests, and I burst out laughing as I unlock my car.

"No. That sounds like a sexual innuendo or something. How about Lola and Lennon?" Lola smirks, cocking her head. "It's simple. And we happen to have two L names."

Her lips twist into a smile. "I like it. But what if you trial it and hate it here? And every day, I walk into a shop named after my ex best friend, and the painful reminder becomes too much to bear?"

I swat her arm. "L & L Bakery?"

She winces. "Let's think on it."

I give her a quick peck on the cheek. "Are you sure you don't want to stop by tonight?" I ask, alluding to the party at the house.

She shakes her head. "Remi and I have plans to watch a Disney movie," she groans.

I chuckle. "Okay. I'll tell everyone you say hello."

We say goodbye, and I drive home. Once inside, I hear the echo of voices in the basement. Setting my purse down on the counter, I walk down the winding staircase and find the guys hanging out in the chapel, shirtless after working out.

"How was it?" Silas asks, walking over to me with a towel around his neck. His skin is glistening with sweat, and I swallow as my eyes rove over to Damon and Jude.

"Really nice," I answer with a smile, leaning against a pew.

"Do you think you'll take her up on her offer?" Silas's question is innocent, but I know he's really asking if I'll continue to work at Savage Ink.

I shrug. "We're going to trial it for a couple of months before I sign any papers." His shoulders sag a bit, so I continue. "Just part-time. A couple of days a week. I can still help at Savage four days a week."

I'd done the math in my head, and for some reason, I'd been nervous to cut out two full days at Savage. But I needed to give myself a day off, and there's no way I could work at the bakery and at Savage on the same day, which left four days at the studio and two at the bakery.

It's going to be a crazy summer...

Silas smiles and walks over to me. "Hey, whatever you need. Don't worry about us."

I reach out for him as he envelops me in a hug. Damon and Jude walk up to us. "We were just talking about Liam," Jude interjects.

"Yeah? What crazy ass things is he up to now?"

Jude's face twists into a scowl. "He brought me to a leadership meeting this morning," he starts, and I sit down. "I'm being initiated," he adds, hands in the pockets of his dark grey sweatpants, looking much too casual about this as my stomach drops.

"What does that mean?" I ask nervously, Silas and Damon sitting on either side of me.

"It means that Jude is going to be gone a lot–church business, helping with services, working at their office," Silas chimes in. "I've given him the go ahead, and we're going to figure out how to move some of his appointments so that he's not at Savage full time."

I chew on the inside of my cheek. I hate this. "But what's the point? Can't you get in, grab the stuff we need, and leave?"

Jude shakes his head. "I wish it were that easy. In the meeting today, they alluded to another office space, which is where I believe they house any incriminating evidence. I need to figure out a way to snoop around without getting caught, and then I need to figure out a way to make copies of the evidence without detection."

I nod, not able to help the pout forming on my face. "I guess that makes sense."

"And then Jude is going to take all of those motherfuckers down," Damon growls from beside me.

I look at Jude, and his eyes burn into mine. "Is this safe?"

He laughs, his scowl softening. "Not at all." His eyes find Silas's. "But it'll be worth it if we can pull it off."

If.

I don't like that word, or this conversation. Something niggles at me, but I don't understand why. I'm about to say something when Silas pulls me up and into his arms.

"You look beautiful today," he murmurs, leaning down and placing a soft kiss on my lips.

I pull away, smirking. "It's just an old t-shirt…"

Damon's hand runs along my backside, his fingers grazing the fabric of my jeans. Goosebumps arise along my skin. I know they are distracting me. I am a worrier, and they understand this about me. I twist out of Silas's arms.

"There's something you're not telling me," I accuse, crossing my arms. My eyes find Jude's.

He runs a finger over his mouth. "I promise you, princess. That's all we know. I won't hide things from you."

He cocks his head. "I'm supposed to meet Liam and the other leaders tomorrow morning."

I frown. "I have a bad feeling about all of this."

It's true. For the last couple of weeks, I can't help but wonder if Liam knows we're playing him. He's a smart guy. And Jude seemingly changed his tune on a whim. If I were Liam, I would be skeptical. And now Jude is being initiated so soon? It sounds too good to be true. I open my mouth to tell him, but he takes a step forward, lifting my chin with his hand.

"Lennon, I'll be fine. I can see the worry in your eyes, but I promise you. I'll be fine."

I wrap my arms around his neck, pulling him into a tight hug. I'm desperate for him suddenly–for all of them. Anything could happen to him, to us. And right now? I have three sweaty, hot as fuck men surrounding me. I grind myself against Jude, smirking as my lips graze his.

"Are you instigating something, princess?" he growls into my ear.

I pull away from him and walk over to Silas, grabbing his neck and pulling his head down for a kiss. He moans into my mouth, and I feel him harden against the waistband of my jeans.

"You sure you want us like this, Lennon?" Silas asks, running a finger down the side of my face. "We're all fucked up on adrenaline from lifting. I can't promise that I'll be able to control myself or be gentle."

I look over Silas's shoulder at Damon, who is watching me with that feral gaze I love so much.

"I want you to do whatever you want with me," I tell him softly, bringing my gaze back to Silas, my lust-filled eyes locked right on his.

In a flash, Silas is lifting me, and I squeal as he carries

me to the altar. I try not to think of Briar being down here at some point, doing this exact thing, but Silas makes that an easy feat as he sets me down in front of the giant cross.

"How do you want us, princess?"

I get up on my knees, everything inside of me pulsing with need. I've been with one or two of them separately since the night we all tied Wright up and made him watch our foursome, but this is the first time since then that I get to have them all.

"Silas," I order quietly, gesturing to the floor. My eyes flick between Jude and Damon. "I want you both in my mouth. And then I want Silas inside of me." I slowly unbutton my jeans and pull them off, working my underwear down my legs next. My shirt and bra are off in seconds. "Your turn," I add, nodding to their pants.

In an instant, all three guys have their pants off, and they're watching me hungrily. Silas kneels next to me, fisting the back of my hair and pulling me in for a rough kiss. I let out a low moan, and then he's lying down and clawing at my thighs to straddle him. Moving one knee to the other side of his torso, I lower myself on top of him, sliding myself slowly along his shaft. He lets out a hiss, grabbing the flesh of my hips and grinding against me. I smile and feel for his cock just as his hands come up to cup my breasts. Raising myself up slightly, I come back down onto his length slowly until he bottoms out.

"I fucking love your pussy," Silas growls. Jude and Damon walk over, each of them already stroking their cocks. Silas twists my nipples as he moves me up and down his shaft, coating his cock in my arousal. "I love how wet you get for us," he adds, using one finger to spread my wetness around. He then brings his hand to his mouth, sucking on his finger, and a spark of heat flares through me.

I reach out for Damon and Jude, taking their monster cocks in each of my hands. I run my fingers along Jude's piercings, and then I bend forward, taking him in my mouth while I stroke Damon's cock and move on top of Silas at the same time. It takes some coordination, and I finally give up.

"Can you both stand in front of me?" I ask Damon and Jude. "Side by side?" I see them look at each other before moving to stand over Silas, who continues to pump into me.

Reaching out, I direct both of them into my mouth, and Damon hisses.

"Fuck, Lennon," he says quickly, sliding his cock against Jude's.

My lips stretch to accommodate, but I'm not able to take them both into the back of my throat, instead focusing on the heads with my lips and tongue. My spit lubes them up, and they use each other for friction. Groaning, Silas drives into me, his hips slapping my thighs as he fucks me from the floor.

I feel Silas grip the flesh of my sides tighter, thrusting into me so that I can concentrate on taking Jude and Damon in my mouth. I close my eyes, letting the feeling of my full mouth overtake me. Someone's hand comes around my throat.

"Good girl," Jude purrs, and I moan. He slowly lets go, and when I look up at them, I see Damon grab Jude's face, kissing him.

Fuck.

I take a break and pull them out of my mouth, using my hands as I look down at Silas. He's watching me with awe, his brows furrowed and his tongue moving inside his cheek in concentration. I roll my hips, meeting his every thrust as my hands work Damon and Jude, and his eyes darken as he ups the tempo, our bodies slapping together.

"Fuck, Lennon," he rasps, his voice hoarse.

He slows down, moving me up and then slamming me back down. His cock fills me, and I feel myself getting close to climaxing, clenching around his thickness. I pull Jude and Damon back into my mouth with hunger, and my clit throbs when I feel them both start to fuck my mouth in tandem, using each other as they fervently kiss above me. Their bodies writhe against me, against each other, and *fuck*, this feels so fucking good.

I whimper when Silas drives into me even harder, over and over, his hips grinding up into mine with each rough, measured thrust. His hands rove over my taut nipples, squeezing them and making me cry out. I arch my back, feeling all my muscles begin to tense up, my clit swollen and needy. I'm moving with every thrust, and drool dribbles down my chin as Jude and Damon begin to quicken their pace, chasing their orgasms.

I take them out of my mouth again. "I want you both inside of me next," I say, and I smile as they continue to kiss, groaning in unison at my demand. Looking down at Silas, I bend down and kiss him, and one of his hands comes to the back of my hair, gripping me tightly.

"I could do this every fucking day for the rest of my life, Lennon Rose," he growls. "Every fucking second."

Feeling the same way, I moan into his mouth as I ride him, moving my hips with a renewed, animalistic pace before sitting up, placing my palms on his chest.

"Soak me, princess. I want you to come all over me."

His words snap something inside of me, and suddenly, I'm barreling toward my climax. My pussy contracts around him, and I feel his cock harden inside of me.

"Oh, fuck," he groans, fire alighting his eyes as he watches me lose control, and I whimper in response.

My orgasm thunders through me. My whole body begins to shake as I squeeze my eyes shut, electric shocks pulsing within me as I scream out with no abandon. I can feel him filling me, his cock twitching with every spurt of come. I gasp for air as I rock my twitching hips through my release and collapse against his chest, trying to catch my breath. I climb off him and look over at Jude and Damon, who are locked in a tight embrace, grinding their bodies against each other.

Damon pulls away, looking at me with hooded eyes. "Lie down, Lennon."

twenty

Silas

I watch as Lennon lies down on the floor of the altar, her pussy still slick with my come. Even though I just spilled inside of her, I feel my cock begin to grow again as Damon lies down next to her and maneuvers her on top of him, her back to his chest.

"I want to try something," he growls, the tip of his erection teasing her entrance. I reach down and begin to stroke my cock, watching as my friend teases her, rubbing his cock along her slit to lube himself up. "Jude, climb on top of her," Damon adds, his voice commanding.

Jude hovers over Lennon, and she looks over at me–her face serious. I crawl over to them and watch as Damon pushes into her. She gasps, taking him in fully. Jude then rubs his length against Damon, using his hand to push into her pussy.

"Oh fuck," she whimpers, a hand flying to her mouth as Jude's cock slips into her above Damon's. "Oh my God, I'm so full," she moans out, spreading her legs wider as Damon fucks her pussy from below her, and Jude fucks her pussy from above.

I'm working my cock quickly now, watching as my friends stretch and tease her, as their hard cocks rub against each other. I kneel next to Lennon's head.

Lennon looks at me and gives me a lazy smile. "Again?"

I pull my lower lip between my teeth. "Like I said... I could fuck you every second of every day and never get enough of you, Lennon." I position myself over her chest. She must read my mind, because she opens her mouth for me instead.

Fuck. Me.

The way Jude and Damon are both fucking her senseless now, their movements desperate, I know they're close. And then Lennon makes a noise in the back of her throat, closing her eyes, and I know she's about to come again, too.

"I'm coming," Jude hisses.

A second later, Damon grunts a strangled, "Fuck."

I feel my balls tighten, and then I reach down and put one hand around her neck, pushing my cock inside her cherry red lips.

"Fuck, your mouth feels so fucking good," I groan.

My cock jumps inside her mouth as her tongue swirls around the head. She begins to moan around my cock, and I see her pussy spray Jude and Damon, her body convulsing between them as come seeps out of her. Grunting, I squeeze her neck tighter and look down at her. She nods, giving me permission, and I thrust deep into the back of her throat, causing her eyes to water.

"You feel me?" I ask, thrusting deeper. My head hits the back of her throat, but my little princess doesn't even gag, she just bobs her head to take me in deeper. "I want to feel my cock in your throat, so deep you still feel me tomorrow," I add, squeezing her soft skin even tighter.

She moans around my length, needy for me. Damon and Jude pull out of her, and I watch as a massive amount of come spills out of her shining pussy. I throw my head back and use her neck to guide her head, driving my hips into the back of her throat. I cry out as I erupt inside of her mouth just seconds later, feeling her swallow my come with each surge that spills down her throat. My cock pulses in her mouth, and I feel it jump against the hand around her neck. When I'm finished, I pull out, and she gasps for air. Looking up at me, she smiles.

"I definitely want to do *that* again," she purrs, like the good girl that she is for us.

twenty-one

Lennon

After I shower and clean up, the four of us make a quick dinner before Briar and her partners show up. They've agreed to get inked by the guys, and I'm weirdly excited at the prospect of meeting all of them, since Ledger–Silas's brother–is the only one I've officially met. I throw on a leather miniskirt and a white, sleeveless bodysuit. Deciding to let my hair dry naturally, so that the waves are a bit wild, I then step into black boots. I swipe some nude lipstick on, and then head downstairs, where I hear voices echoing from the foyer.

Taking the stairs slowly, I crane my neck around to the front of the house, spying Briar and four very handsome men.

I see Ledger, whom I've already met. Next to him is a man in a suit, who looks slightly out of place with his serious expression and expensive watch. He's smiling warmly at Briar, and I can feel the love for her radiating off him. To his right is another man–he looks familiar, but I can't quite put my finger on why. I've seen his face before. He's wearing a black button-up, and he glances around the house like he owns the place, his hands in his pockets and a cocky expression on his face. Behind him is the fourth guy, with longer hair, a brooding expression, and a plain white tee-shirt. His eyes meet mine, and he gives me a heart-stopping smile.

Interesting.

The dynamic seems to be all over the place, and I can't wait to meet them all officially. Walking into the foyer, I smile at Briar and give her a hug.

"You look gorgeous," she comments, running a hand over my long, blonde hair.

"Likewise." She's in a long, flowing red dress, and her hair is braided into a crown atop her head.

"Where's Easton?" I ask, looking around.

Briar gives me a mischievous grin. "My mom has him tonight." She looks at the guy in a white t-shirt. "Her husband–Hunter's father–is nearing sixty, so the joke's on them, I guess."

My eyes find Hunter's. *Ah, the stepbrother.* I reach a hand out, and he shakes it. "So we finally meet," he says, his voice low and sensual.

"So we do," I respond, giving Briar a look that I hope says, *I don't blame you for banging your stepbrother.*

I'm introduced to her other partners. Samson is the one in a suit. I learn that he's an environmental engineer. He's a little more soft-spoken than the others, but the way he looks at Briar is just adorable. Apparently, Hunter is a famous writer, which makes sense given his more laid-back style. And the last guy? The one I thought I recognized from somewhere? It's Ash Greythorn–the fucking *mayor* of Greythorn. I'd seen a few of his older posters around town, but they really do not do him justice at all.

Once the seven guys head into the kitchen for beers, I pull Briar aside.

"Okay, I'm officially jealous of you," I joke, linking arms with her as we slowly trail our partners through the house.

She laughs. "It could be you one day, Lennon."

I shake my head as we walk into the kitchen. Silas hands me a beer, winking at me before he walks away. My stomach dips. I feel like a giddy schoolgirl around all of them. Will that always be the case? I watch as Hunter hands Briar a glass of wine, and the look they share is pure companionship–and love. I grew up watching people fall into monogamous relationships, so it's nice to see how a polyamorous relationship can work in the real world. I suppose it happens like any other relationship–sparks fly in the honeymoon phase, but then real life sets in, and you have to navigate not one, but *multiple* relationships. The thought is both daunting and exciting.

We all head downstairs, and I watch as Silas, Damon, and Jude begin to set up their workstations on the pews. All five of them are getting something done, and yet they have no idea what tattoos will forever be etched onto their skin. I vow to let the guys tattoo me again–and to see what else they come up with besides the logo of their shop. I'd love for them to ink me permanently with their art.

Silas takes Ledger, and I can tell from the look they share that whatever Silas inks on him will be meaningful. They look *so* much alike, it's almost like I'm looking at twins. Damon takes Briar, and she gives me a nervous look before scooting over to him. Jude takes Hunter. Samson and Ash plop down on either side of me.

SAVAGE GODS

"Hi," I say casually, but I see them glance at me and then at each other.

"We have to thank you," Ash says, his voice low as he leans closer to me. We're far enough away from everyone that I know they won't be able to hear our conversation. "Ever since you and Briar had coffee, she seems happier."

I don't expect them to say that. I look over at him, and he's watching Damon as he disinfects the skin on Briar's shoulder.

"It was really nice," I answer. "I'm glad we met."

Samson sighs from the other side of me. "It's been rough on her. She had an easy pregnancy and birth, but motherhood really took a toll."

I nod. "I can imagine."

Ash leans forward, his chin resting on his hand. "Being a parent, and especially a co-parent, means you really have to dig deep and pull from the reservoirs of your soul, you know? And for us, we were together for years before we tried for Easton. The excitement was gone. We were just a regular poly couple, living our lives. They don't tell you that, though. And it was hard for Briar, because she didn't feel worthy of us. She felt like a shell of herself."

"I think seeing you helped her to remember who she was before Easton, and even before us," Samson adds, and he shares a look with Ash. "After the coffee with you, she seemed… lighter. And we realized it's because you're the first friend, aside from us, that she's had in years."

I swallow the lump in my throat. Not only is Briar wonderful, but her partners are so aware of her needs. If I chose to have children with Silas, Damon, and Jude, would they know these things about me? Would they seek out things that make me happy, like Samson and Ash are doing? My gut tells me they would. Because Ash is right–one day, the sex will stop being new, and the excitement of being with three guys will wear off. And where will that leave us? Would we be strong enough to withstand that?

Damon finishes Briar, and she trots over, showing off the gorgeous 'E' on her shoulder.

"For Easton," she mumbles, and Ash pulls her into a tight hug. "I told Damon he could do whatever he wanted, and, well..." she trails off, her eyes watery. "It's perfect."

Samson goes next, and then Hunter walks back over to where we're all seated. Silas, Damon, and Jude all finish up their designs, and we drink beer until the early hours of the morning. We say goodbye, walking them out to their car, and then the four of us head upstairs. I like the feel of Damon's arm around my shoulder, and Jude's arm around my waist.

For a second, I consider what it would be like to stay in Greythorn–to stay in this house, in this town, forever. Before, I felt dread. But now? It wouldn't be the worst thing in the world.

I'd have the bakery.

I'd have friends.

But most importantly, I'd have the guys.

Damon and Silas say goodnight, and Jude gives me a quick peck on the cheek. I grab his hand, pulling him closer.

"Be careful tomorrow," I plead. I haven't stopped thinking about it.

Jude brushes my cheek with the pad of his thumb. "I'll be back before breakfast, princess."

He gives me a soft kiss, and then he's gone, and I'm left with the same empty, uneasy feeling as earlier today.

twenty-two

Lennon

Just as I'm climbing into bed, there's a knock on my bedroom door.

"Come in."

Silas walks in and shuts the door behind him. He's only wearing a black t-shirt and gray sweatpants. His eyes are wild, emotional, and my pulse speeds up as he walks over to me. I don't say anything as he gets into bed with me.

"You okay?" I ask, turning my light out.

"Didn't feel like sleeping alone," he says, his voice raw.

I know he's not telling me the whole truth. And sometimes I see it on his face–the trauma he endured growing up. I recognize it, because I see it in myself, too. And I know how it can haunt you at night, in the dark. How it finds you when you're alone. I scoot closer to him so that his chest is to my back, and his muscled arm comes around my torso. I'm only wearing an oversized t-shirt and underwear, so his warm skin against mine, even through our clothes, feels nice. My body heats at his touch, and his calloused finger grazes the exposed bit of my abdomen. Goosebumps rise on my skin, spreading to every limb. I hear Silas chuckle in my ear.

"What's so funny?" I whisper, unconsciously arching my back and moving my ass into his hips.

"Nothing," he whispers back, his tone amused.

"Tell me," I demand, rocking my hips slightly against him.

Suddenly, he places a firm hand on my ass, stopping me from moving. "Stop doing that, Lennon, unless you want me to rip these panties right off you."

"And if I do?" I taunt, knowing I'm pushing his buttons.

"I came here to sleep," he growls. "And to cuddle."

I snort. "To cuddle?!"

He unexpectedly sits up and hovers over me, his hands on either side of my arms. I can barely make out his face, but by the way he's breathing heavily, I know he's either pissed off or…

"Yes. To cuddle." His voice is low and rough. The sound raises the temperature between us, heat licking my skin as he looks down at me.

"I didn't take you for a cuddler," I tease, biting my lip to keep from smiling too wide.

"We're not cuddling now," he asserts with narrowed eyes, slamming his lips against mine.

I raise my hips and wrap my legs around him, pulling him closer. He grinds against me, nipping and biting the delicate skin along my neck.

"I feel like an animal around you," he snarls, and I can't help the moan that escapes me as his lips completely overwhelm my senses.

Reaching down, he fists my lace underwear and rips it off. "Hey! Those were my favorite—"

"Be quiet," he hisses, and I hear him lower his sweatpants. The head of his cock rubs against my clit, and I whimper, moving my hips against him.

"Please," I beg, already breathless.

Without warning, he drives into me as I gasp. "I really did come in here to sleep," he retorts, his voice ragged. Pulling out slowly, he slams back in. *Hard.* Bottoming out against my cervix, I reach up for the headboard, keeping myself steady as he pulls out and thrusts back in.

"You like it when I'm rough?" he growls, reaching down and throwing one of my legs over his shoulder.

"Oh God," I cry, squeezing my eyes shut as he pounds me. He's stretching me and filling me so completely, the hard head of his cock rubbing the perfect spot inside of me to make me tense up. "Harder," I whisper, bucking my hips against him to get more friction. "Fuck," I moan, fisting the bed sheets as Silas drives into me, over and over. His hand squeezes my thigh roughly, spreading my legs wide as he looks down between us.

"I love your pussy," he rasps, moving in and out slowly now, watching where we're joined.

He reaches over and grabs a pillow, lifting my hips, placing it underneath my ass. I'm not sure what changes with that one small movement, but it does something to the angle of his cock inside of me, and I whimper as I feel something powerful building in my core.

"Holy fuck," I gasp, my voice frayed.

Silas circles his hips ever so slightly, making sure the head of his hard shaft hits the same spot inside of me every time. Everything sounds so wet now, the sound of my arousal echoing around the room. I can feel my pussy grip his firm length like a vise, squeezing it until something explodes out of me. I completely reject his cock at that point, my body convulsing as something sprays Silas. At first, I think I must be peeing, but then as my climax rolls through me, more powerful than ever, I realize it can only be one thing.

"That's it, baby," Silas grunts, his hand working the shaft of his cock quickly as he watches me soak him. "I want every last drop."

My body shakes and trembles underneath him, and as soon as I'm done, he thrusts back into me, using my wetness as lube.

"Holy fucking shit," he growls, his voice uneven. "Your soaked pussy is going to make me come." I arch my back as he slows his thrusting. "Watch me fill you, Lennon," he commands, and then he groans loudly.

I look between us as his cock pulses inside of me, and I can feel each powerful rope of come hit my cervix. I shift my hips up and down, squeezing every last drop out of him as he twitches and spasms, his fingers digging into my thighs. Finally, when he's done, he lowers himself on top of me, kissing my sweaty brow.

"That's never happened before," I say, alluding to the way I rejected him and completely sprayed him.

"Yes, it has," he answers, kissing the tip of my nose. "In the shop. The night Jude was inside of you. There have been other times, too, but I don't think you notice."

I smile at that. "Well, I guess you know I'm not faking it."

He grunts in response, trailing a finger up between my breasts. "I can tell without needing to see you come, Lennon. For one, your chest gets flushed," he murmurs, his rough fingers grazing the sensitive skin of my collarbone.

"Sometimes your eyes roll into the back of your head, and your toes?" He smirks, kissing my temple. "They curl, like you're half in pain."

I moan as he continues to ply me with kisses. After a few minutes, I start to get sleepy, so I use the restroom and then climb back into bed with him. He must've changed the sheets and cleaned up the bed while I was gone, because the bed is freshly made and dry. I snuggle up to him, grabbing his arm and wrapping it around my midsection.

"I think I love you, Silas Huxley," I mumble, sleep finding me before I have a chance to hear his response.

twenty-three

Lennon

I wake up late the next morning. The sun is already high in the sky, and my room is warm and hazy. Silas is gone–probably to work out–so I get ready for the day. As I'm washing my hair, I can't help but shake the uneasy feeling deep inside my gut. Something is wrong, I can sense it. I don't bother drying my hair or putting on makeup, instead pulling on an old pair of jeans and a simple tank top. Checking my phone, I head down. It's nearly eleven in the morning. I turn the corner of the stairwell, stopping when I see Silas and Damon sitting in the living room.

Instantly, I know something is *really* wrong.

"Jude." I rush toward them. "Where is he?"

Silas stands up and grabs both of my arms. "Lennon, it's okay. Sit down."

I shake my head, bile rising in my throat. I can't seem to control the panic flooding my body, and my hands begin to tremble.

"Where is Jude?" I demand. My eyes flick between each of their somber faces.

"He didn't come home," Damon explains. Sighing, he stands and walks over to me. "We think he's still at the meeting with the Church leadership, but he turned his phone off."

Or someone else did.

I cover my mouth and try to calm my racing heart. "We have to call the cops," I say quickly. "They could *hurt* him, or–"

"Not until he's been missing for twenty-four hours," Silas explains. "Until then... we have to wait. And hope it's all just a misunderstanding."

I nod slowly. "Okay. Yeah, sure, maybe he's just shooting the shit with them." I pace the living room. "When did he leave?"

"Seven," Damon answers.

Four hours. He's been gone for *four* hours.

My breathing turns ragged, and Silas pulls me into his chest. "Hey, it's okay. We're going to find him. He could walk through the front door at any minute."

"He'd get a kick out of us being so worried." Damon chuckles.

I force myself to laugh, but inside, I feel sick. Wringing my hands together, I pace in front of the door for what feels like forever. Damon brings me a cup of coffee, and Silas forces me to eat some toast. I try calling Jude a million times, and each time, it goes to voicemail. I don't even let myself think about the worst-case scenario–after all, a world without Jude Vanderbilt feels empty and hollow. I need him. I *love* him. Nothing bad can happen to him.

"What if we go by the church?" I ask an hour later, my

voice hopeful. "Maybe his car is there, and we can just see that he's inside."

Silas shakes his head. "It would blow his cover. Liam thinks he's lying to us. We have to pretend not to know. At least for now. We can outwardly worry later if he misses his appointments."

I nervously chew on the inside of my cheek. "But what if he's hurt?" My voice is softer than I intend it to be, and Damon looks down at the floor, scowling.

"If they hurt him, every last one of them is going to die," he mutters, his voice a low growl.

"So we just have to pretend life is normal until later, or even tomorrow?"

Silas nods. "We need to reschedule his appointments tonight just in case–"

I hold a hand out, stopping him. "Hold on. We're *working* tonight?"

Damon walks over to me, taking my hands. "Princess, I know this is hard. Trust me. It's eating me up inside. But if Liam suspects we know, then he will have someone reporting back to him about whether or not we're open tonight. He might actually hurt Jude if he hasn't done so already."

If he hasn't done so already.

I pull Damon in for a hug, feeling Silas's arms wrap around both of us. "We will find him," Silas utters, and I feel him grip my shirt. Damon's arms squeeze me tightly, and I let myself cry. Just for a minute.

Jude has to be okay.

He *has* to be, because I can't imagine the alternative.

―――

Despite being beside myself with worry, I throw on a pair of boots and a black cardigan before heading to Savage Ink with the guys. I manage to call every single one of Jude's clients and let them know he's sick, and we reschedule them for a later date. The drive to town is melancholy, and the three of us don't really speak until we get inside of Savage. I know we're all thinking the worst. By the time Silas parks a few blocks away, I'm actively trying to hold back the tears.

"What if they–"

"Lennon," Silas says, his voice low so that no one overhears us.

"But won't Liam's people be suspicious if we *don't* act worried? Our friend is missing. We should be freaking out."

Damon sighs, pulling me off the sidewalk to show me something on his phone. It's a text from Jude. It's timestamped 9:07am.

Hey, I need time to think some things over. I'm going to Boston, and I don't know when I'll be back.

I look up at Damon, curling my fists at my sides as my eyes flick between him and Silas.

"Why are you just now showing this to me?"

Damon shrugs. "I didn't think anything of it. I thought maybe he got sucked into some weird Church of the Rapture trip and wouldn't be able to communicate." I cross my arms and wait for him to elaborate. "I know he sent it with Liam watching over his shoulder. Or maybe Liam sent it himself. My point is, the Church thinks we think he's off somewhere for some mental health shit. If we start acting worried, they will know."

I look between them. Silas is frowning, his hand propped on the wall next to me, and Damon is breathing heavily, his brows furrowed in concern.

"Okay, I understand the reason we're *supposed* to think he's gone. And if anyone comes sniffing around to watch us, I will pretend nothing is amiss," I add, holding my head up high. "But I can't believe we're not doing anything about it. He could be hurt. He could be locked up somewhere."

"Or," Silas counters, "he could *actually* be away with the Church. I don't think we should panic until we haven't heard anything by tomorrow morning."

They usher me back onto the sidewalk, toward Savage Ink, but I don't say anything. I *can't*. I know they all had a plan before I even showed up. And I know they would never intentionally let anything bad happen to him. I just wish I could guarantee that he was okay somehow–with my own two eyes.

The night passes slowly, and every few minutes, I catch myself checking my phone, or glancing at the front door of Savage, and any time I see Silas or Damon, I ask them if they've heard anything–to which they always say no. Around eight, there's a lull in clients coming in, so I dig around the internet a bit. I read the Wikipedia page for Church of the Rapture, and then I find a few articles from ex members who've come forward with accusations against the church. I pull one of them up, skimming the text, but nothing hugely incriminating comes up.

I scroll through Instagram to distract myself, and my heart drops into my stomach when I see a new post from Church of the Rapture. It's an image of an underground cave, with one line of text:

We are punished by our sins, not for them.

Sitting up straighter, I open an internet browser and Google Church of the Rapture + underground cave. Hundreds of articles come up, and my mouth opens when I read one of them.

Samuel Kent–aka the Boston Baptist–founded Church of the Rapture in the early 1990s. His early followers were few and far between, but they were loyal–so loyal that the church soon grew to over five hundred members in the Boston area by the year 2006. The church, –whose main purpose is to prepare for the inevitable ascension to Heaven to meet God, was once housed in a rural, underground cave northeast of Boston. The rock his followers worshiped, which was believed to be a holy site, was recently desecrated. As of 2003, no one has seen or heard from Samuel Kent.

I look up as Silas saunters over, and I click out of the browser. "Tell me more about Samuel Kent." I hear Damon's needle stop for just a second, telling me this is not something Silas is going to want to talk about.

"Lennon..."

I stand up, and I see Damon set his tattoo gun down. "What about the cave? You never told me what happened to Samuel Kent," I whisper. "What if he has something to do with Jude's disappearance?"

Sure, I may be grasping at straws here, but the fact that their Instagram has a picture of an underground cave, along with an ominous quote, on the same day Jude goes missing? Yeah, maybe I'm not grasping at straws at all. I need to know *everything*. Maybe one tiny detail can save Jude's life.

Silas must see the resolute look on my face, because he mutters something to his client, who is lying face down, then grabs me by the arm, pulling me into the bathroom. She's getting her entire back done tonight, and I'm sure he's giving her a much-needed break from the pain.

"Jesus, Lennon," Silas growls, shutting and locking the door behind him. "What does Samuel Kent have to do with Jude?"

I pull my phone out of my back pocket, showing him

the picture and caption. Maybe I'm imagining it, but I swear I see his face go slightly pale.

"Samuel Kent worshiped in those caves, right? So it's not a stretch to put two and two together," I hiss. "What if they took him to the caves, Silas? Do you know where they are?"

Silas grimaces and nods, running a hand through his hair. "Yeah. I know where they are."

I wait for him to elaborate, but he just sighs, leaning against the tiled wall. "We need to find him. He's been gone all day, and I'm going out of my mind with worry."

Silas's eyes darken. "You think I'm not? Fuck, Lennon, he's my best friend. I'm sick to my fucking stomach with worry. And then you go and show me this shit."

"Tell me about Samuel Kent," I growl. "There's something you're not telling m–"

"He molested me."

My blood cools, and I feel my stomach begin to roll with nausea. "What?"

Silas rubs his face with his hands. "I was ten. Samuel was over, and it... happened. I can't go into detail, Lennon, because I'm still trying to process it–"

I lunge forward and pull him into a hug. "I'm so, so sorry." Squeezing my eyes shut, burning with unshed tears, I fist the back of his shirt as he hugs me back. First Samuel, and then Liam... Jesus. No wonder he hated the church so much.

"I was ten. My parents caught him. They threw him out and never spoke to him again. He fled after that, and no one has seen him since." He pauses, and I can hear him thinking. "It was the one good thing they ever did for me."

A shiver works down my spine. "Silas, I had no idea. Do the guys know?"

Silas nods against my head. "I told them right after it happened."

Their bond has been strong since he was ten, strong enough to confide in each other about something like that. Strong enough to love each other in more ways than one. Strong enough for them to share me. I squeeze Silas tighter. *How did I get so lucky?*

Suddenly, it becomes clear to me.

Jude is missing, and Silas has a history with the church. Damon needs to stay behind and keep us all in check with his authoritative nature. But me?

"Where is this cave?" I ask casually, as I pull back to look up at him.

Silas loosens his hold, his brows knitting together as he looks down at me. "Why?"

I shrug. "I didn't realize Massachusetts had an underground cave."

He smirks. "It's somewhere up on the northeast side of the state. It's hard to find. I'd have to explain it."

Okay, so he's going to make it hard for me.

I nod. "If we file a missing person's report, we should probably tell the cops about it."

"Yeah. That's true."

He places a lingering kiss on my temple, and I sigh in his embrace before unlocking the bathroom door and heading back out to the studio. Silas wanders back to his client, and I don't make eye contact with Damon.

I'm afraid of what he'll see.

I check the clock. Eight-fifteen. I grab my purse. "While it's slow, I'm going to grab a pizza from down the street," I announce. "Anyone want anything?"

This isn't completely unusual. I have gone out to grab

dinner before, though Silas usually orders delivery on the nights that we need real food.

I look at Damon, and he gives me a soft smile. My heart clenches–he has no idea. When I look at Silas, he's distracted and helping his client. They both shake their heads, so I quickly walk out before they catch on.

I get a few blocks away when I find a lone taxi waiting near The Queens Arms. The driver turns around and faces me as I close the door.

"Where are you headed, miss?"

I give him our address, and while I'm at it, I google the Boston Baptist cave. A map appears, along with directions. It's going to be dark out, so I'll need a flashlight. Zooming in on the map, I estimate it's about two miles from the nearest road. Doubt begins to slither into my mind. *What am I doing? Why am I heading into a forest by myself? I can't just leave Damon and Silas alone with their clients...*

But then I imagine someone hurting Jude.

Maybe someone *already* hurt Jude, and he needs our help.

I swallow the bile creeping up my throat. I can't imagine anything bad happening to him, and I'd do the same for any of the guys.

If Silas and Damon refuse to save Jude, I'll have to do it myself.

And something tells me Jude is in those caves, waiting for us to find him.

twenty-four

Damon

The clock shows eight-thirty, and there are a few people clustered around the front desk now for my next appointment. I really fucking hate it when people bring their family to tattoo appointments. They always have something to say, some way of interjecting themselves into the situation. I understand that some people may need moral support, but I don't need Aunt Eunice to tell my client what does and doesn't look good.

Let me be the judge of that.

I ignore the nervous rumble of my stomach. When I look over at Silas, his expression tells me everything I need to know. After I get my client and her cousins all settled in–*kill me now*–I walk over to Silas's station. He's still working on Roberta's back, and it looks fucking rad. Motioning for me to follow him to the back, I glance one more time at the front door.

"Did Lennon say where she was going?" Silas asks, running a nervous hand through his hair.

I shake my head.

"Fuck."

"What did you tell her?" I ask, crossing my arms. "When she asked about Samuel Kent, I mean."

Silas chews on the inside of his cheek. "I told her the truth."

The door jingles, but it's just another client for me. We both sigh nervously.

"Want me to check the pizza place for her?"

Silas looks at me and nods. "It couldn't hurt."

I walk back over to my clients and explain that I need to run a few doors down quickly. Fortunately, all seven family members are understanding.

When I get outside, a cool breeze blows against my face, and goosebumps erupt on my skin. *Fuck.* Where could she be? Does it have anything to do with Jude?

I walk inside the pizza shop, but it's empty of customers. One lone man is sitting behind the counter reading a newspaper.

"Have you seen my partner?" I ask the man behind the counter. "A woman, tall, blonde… have you seen anyone like that in the last half hour?"

He narrows his eyes. "We haven't had anyone in since seven," he mutters, scowling. "Damn game," he adds, gesturing to the sports game on the television.

"Okay, thanks."

My pulse rushes in my ears as I pull my phone out of my pocket and dial her number.

"Fuck." Straight to voicemail.

I growl, resisting the urge to throw my phone against the ground. Instead, I jog back into Savage, shaking my head when Silas looks up at me. He mutters something to all the clients, assuring them we've had an emergency, I'm sure. I walk over to my clients and explain the situation–that we're short two staff members and we now have a family emergency on our hands–and they kindly agree to let me reschedule them for some time next month. After they're gone, Silas and I begin to seal up Roberta's back, and she looks relieved when we tell her that we have to close early tonight. Silas promises to get her in soon to finish.

Once she's gone, I turn to face Silas. "What the fuck is going on?" I ask, my voice rougher than I intended.

He scowls as he paces in front of Lennon's desk. "She said she was getting pizza."

I scoff. "Obviously, she lied. Did she say anything about Jude?"

"Fuck," Silas mutters. He slams a fist on the desk, and Lennon's perfectly organized tray falls over on its side. "Fuck!"

"Whoa, what the fuck, man?"

Silas rubs the bridge of his nose. "The caves. She's going to the caves."

I rear my head back. "*Samuel's* caves?" I ask incredulously.

Silas nods grimly. "She'd asked me about them–where they were. I think she thinks Jude is there."

I take a deep breath to calm the fury roiling up inside of me. "What the fuck are we doing here, then? Let's fucking go!"

twenty-five

Lennon

I manage to shove things into a backpack in under ten minutes, running into the kitchen and refilling two large water bottles in case I get lost. I grab some food, and then I leave a note on the kitchen counter, though I suspect once Silas and Damon figure out what I've done, they'll head straight to the cave. Locking up the house, I climb into my car and start the engine.

I drive by the church first, but all the lights are out. I've never been one to believe in intuition, but my gut is screaming at me that Jude isn't here at the church. Turning around quickly, I get onto the highway, headed north. The directions seem easy. It's thirty miles on this road, and then I exit and take another road five miles west. From there, I should see signs for the campground, and that's where I can park. I spend the entire drive calming my nerves and hoping that Silas and Damon won't kill me once they find out where I've gone.

I also have to take into consideration that I might run into Liam at some point tonight. And I've already thought of an excuse to exonerate Jude: I was worried about my friend, which led me to do research on the church. At this point, Jude's been missing for twelve hours. He missed his appointments at the studio, which is very unlike him. So I took things into my own hands. Of course, Liam may be totally off his rocker, and I might be putting myself in just as much danger as Jude, but I haven't let myself think about that yet.

Once I get to the campground parking lot, there are a few other people around. I pretend to be on my phone in my car until they're gone. Once they are, I grab my jacket and backpack, heading down the trailhead that points to "Caverns." It's dark out now, and my flashlight does a great job lighting the way. The trail is open, and the crickets make me feel a bit at peace, despite what I'm about to do. I screenshot the map of the cavern that leads to the area where the Boston Baptist used to hang out, just in case I lose service. I pass a couple of people, but I suppose in an outdoor area like this one, a woman hiking alone in the dark isn't that strange. If one of my friends did this, I'd yell at them, but here I am...

I swallow the fear creeping over me the form of goosebumps. Slowing down, I take a few steadying breaths. Maybe I should turn around? I shine the light behind me, and only dark forest lights up. Ahead of me, the same thing. I suddenly feel completely out of my element. What if I get lost in here, or I die of dehydration? I brought water, but it's not enough to last more than a day. Or worse, what if this is a trap? What if the picture of the cave on Instagram was supposed to lure us out here for a reason?

A twig snaps behind me, and I whirl around, shining

the light in the direction the noise came from. Another snap, though I don't see anything. *God, what if I get eaten by a wild animal?* I start to walk back in the direction I came. This was a bad idea. The hairs on the back of my neck stick up when I see something in my peripheral. Yelping, I shine the light on whatever moved, and then I scream when I feel a hand clamp down on my mouth, pulling me against a firm body.

twenty-six

Silas

"You better be thankful it's just us, princess," I growl into her ear, making her shiver, then let her go, and she spins around with wide eyes. I can't help but laugh at the outrage on her face.

"How the hell did you–"

"You'd make a really fucking terrible spy," Damon adds, his low chuckle echoing against the dense forest.

"What about your clients, and the studi–" Her hands are waving about in frustration, her nose scrunching.

"Well," I muse, taking her flashlight as I lead her back toward the cave, "when one of your employees goes missing, you close up shop and go find her. I figured this is where you were headed, and then I saw your car parked at the campsite." Her shocked expression morphs into a glower as she crosses her arms and takes a deep breath. "Did you really think you could find Jude by yourself?"

She stops and turns to face me, snatching her flashlight

back, her stubborn expression still firmly in place. "You didn't seem that worried, so I thought I'd get a head start."

I sigh and run a hand through my hair. "Lennon, I'm worried shitless. So is Damon. I've had a bad feeling since you showed me that Instagram post. But that doesn't mean I want to come out here by myself in the middle of nowhere, *at night*, and hunt for Jude and the other insane members of the church."

She makes a noise but continues walking forward. Damon sidles up to my side, chuckling, as Lennon strides ahead of us.

"I told you she was going to be pissed," he says, amusement in his voice.

I smile. "Yeah, well, why the hell she would want to do this alone is beyond me."

"Imagine if we didn't find her on time... she would've given Liam a run for his money."

The thought makes me uncomfortable. I clear my throat. "Well, it's a good thing we're with her now. There's no telling what that psycho would do to her."

We all continue for another mile and a half, my flashlight lighting up the path ahead. When we get close to where I think the caves are located, I tell Lennon to turn her flashlight off. Lucky for us, it's a full moon, and the tree cover is a lot less dense in this part of the forest. We can see easily once our eyes adjust.

I've been here once before, with Ledger. It was after he and his friends decimated the rock Samuel Kent used as an altar, and we vowed that day that we'd do whatever we could to take the church down. I decided not to let him in on our plan with Jude going undercover. With a new baby to care for, it didn't feel right to drag him into this. Though I know if he finds out, he's going to skin me alive. He may be my younger brother, but he's just as big as me, and probably stronger, considering he runs like twelve miles a day.

"We should have a plan," Lennon whispers, and I can tell we're close because up ahead of us is a large, rocky face that I recognize as the entrance to the infamous caverns.

I snort, lifting a brow. "Didn't you have a plan when you decided to trek here all by yourself?"

She scowls at me again, and I can't help but laugh because she's cute when she's pissed. "I was winging it," she admits. "I have a map of the underground caves on my phone."

"Then you lead the way, princess."

She smirks, turning quickly and heading into the caves with zero hesitation. I have no doubt that if Liam had caught her, she'd fight back with all her might–and probably win.

The instant we enter the dark, damp caves, I regret our decision. It's about twenty degrees cooler here, and there's zero light, so Lennon has no choice but to use a flashlight. I decide to walk ahead of her, and I tell Damon to stay behind with her in case I bump into Liam, giving them time to run back out into the forest and to safety. I have no idea what lies down here, if anything. There's a good chance Jude isn't even here.

We snake through the cavern, running water trickling every few feet. There's a dirt path, and the walls of the cave are white with minerals and salt from the earth. It's really fucking creepy, and I don't know if I'm shivering from the cold or from what we're about to do. We reconvene a minute later, and Lennon directs us to the left.

"We should find the altar in about three-hundred feet," she whispers.

The silence is unsettling, and I rub my arms to get rid of

the goosebumps prickling on my skin. I hear Lennon whisper something to Damon, and when I round the familiar corner of the altar, I hold my breath. My heart is pounding against my chest, but as I flash the light in every direction, I realize our trek has been futile, because no one is here, and it's clear no one has been here for years. The only evidence of someone being here is an old, rusty can of spray paint. I shine the light down below into the underground river, but nothing. Turning around, I hold my arms out to my sides.

"No one's here."

Lennon looks around, brows furrowed. "I could've sworn he'd be here."

Her voice breaks on the last word, and I realize she thought we were going to rescue Jude. She believed he was here. I pull her into my arms as I stroke her back. "The Instagram post..."

"Maybe it's just a coincidence," Damon chimes in. He peeks behind every crevice and corner, and there's no other way through here.

If no one is in here, no one is in here—we'd have found them. I peek at the rock that Samuel Kent purposed as an altar—a huge slab of stone that used to have drawings on it. They believed Jesus would come to this very cave, and everyone would ascend to Heaven first. Now, it's just a fragmented, cracked surface, and one day soon, I will prove that all of this is a crock of shit.

For my parents. For my brother.

For every victim of this church.

I let Lennon go and we all walk back the way we came. None of us says anything as we wind through the underground cavern. The sound of trickling water is soothing, but in an eerie sort of way, and every few minutes, I swear I hear something or someone. But it's just us in here.

As we exit the cave, Damon wraps an arm around Lennon, and we slowly make our way back to the cars. Disappointment rolls through me, and I ignore the nagging feeling inside. A small part of me hoped we'd find Jude with Lennon's instinct to come here–or at least a clue. The police refuse to file a report until tomorrow morning, so we have to wait until then, and I know none of us are going to sleep well tonight. It's like a limb is missing, and Jude being gone just feels off. Like our entire dynamic is out of whack.

The gravel crunches beneath our feet when we reach the parking lot. According to my phone, it's well past eleven now, and everyone has cleared out of the area. I walk Lennon to her car while Damon starts his, and I bend down to give her a kiss.

"I'm sorry," she says quietly, discouraged. Her eyes find mine, and I see tears pooling in her hazel irises. "I really thought..." she trails off, climbing into the car and placing her hands on the top of the steering wheel. "I thought we'd at least find a clue. A car, maybe a note, something... now we're just back to square one."

"I know," I answer, my voice soft. "How about we check The Queens Arms? You can usually find one of Liam's guys in there on any given night. At least we'll feel like we're doing something."

She nods, and I gesture for Damon to go without me. I see him reverse and leave the parking lot, and then I get into the passenger seat of her car, remembering to shoot him a quick text about our additional stop before heading home. The drive back to Greythorn is quiet, and Lennon turns on Jude's playlist. We're both smiling when the classical music gets intense, knowing Jude loves this shit. We're both in much better moods as we pull into the city center, and she parks in front of the pub. I see Damon pull in next to us. Getting out of the car, we walk up to the front of The Queens Arms, and Lennon pushes the door open.

I run into the back of her body as she stops right inside the door, and before my eyes adjust to the low light, I see her beeline for one of the corners.

"Fuck," Damon mutters.

I squint, and that's when I see him–Liam.

He's sitting in the corner of the bar, working on his laptop.

We rush after her, but not before she slams a fist on the table.

"Where the fuck is he?" she yells, and everyone in the pub quiets.

"Lennon," I warn, pulling her back. "Hey."

She shoves my hand away, and I can tell by Liam's amused face that she's going to rip him apart any second now.

"No, it's fine," Liam says calmly, giving the other patrons a kind smile before standing and coming around the side of the booth.

Lennon reaches out and hits him against the chest. "Where is Jude? Where are you keeping him?"

I pull her away from Liam as he looks between Damon, Lennon, and me. The genuine shock on his face surprises me.

"Just tell us where he is," Damon growls from next to me. "Let's end this stupid fucking game and get on with our lives."

Liam's brows knit together as the people in the pub continue talking, disinterested now that there's not going to be a throwdown.

"I have no idea what you're talking about. What do you mean, where am I keeping him? I dropped him off at the studio after our meeting this morning."

"Bullshit," Lennon hisses. She reaches into her purse and pulls out her phone. "Why the fuck would you post something like this, then?"

"Jude is missing," Damon mumbles. "We haven't seen or heard from him since he left for the meeting this morning."

Liam's eyes flick between all of us again. "I swear to God, I have no idea where he is."

Lennon shoves her phone in his face, and he takes it from her, his eyes scanning the image and words.

"What is this?" he asks, handing the phone back. "Is this a joke?"

Lennon takes a step back. "You tell me. You posted it."

"No, darling. I've never seen that post, or that account."

Lennon scowls up at Liam, not believing him, and I take a step forward.

"Stop fucking with us," I retort, baring my teeth at Liam.

He shakes his head. "It looks like a fan account. The church doesn't have any official social media profiles."

"Then who the fuck has been posting all of this bullshit?" Damon asks, his voice low and menacing. He grabs the phone from Lennon, moving his thumb to refresh the page. His eyes widen, and then he hands the phone to me.

"Fuck," I whisper, nearly dropping the phone.

"What?" Lennon grabs the phone from my hand, and her face goes white. She twists around to Liam. "If you're not the one running this account, then someone else is in our house."

twenty-seven

Lennon

My heart pounds in my chest as we all rush out of The Queens Arms. I hear Silas murmur something to Damon, who basically runs with me to my car. Silas gets into Damon's car. I'm sure they think they're going to keep me from entering the house, but fuck that. I am a part of this group now, just as much as any of them. And if Jude is really in our house, there's a good chance he may be hurt. I *have* to get to him.

"Liam is coming too," Damon says, his tone disapproving, as I reverse out of the parking lot. My hands are shaking as I speed down the main road. I see Damon gripping the side of the door.

"Wonderful," I grit out.

Images of Silas's chapel–the image on the church's Instagram–flash through my mind.

Someone is in our house, and they most likely have Jude.

"Who the hell is doing this if it's not Liam?" I whisper, my rapid breathing not calming down.

Damon shrugs. He places a warm hand on my knee. "We should hold back, let Silas and Liam check out the situation inside–"

I chuckle, my voice a lot crueler than I intend it to be. "Absolutely not."

"Lennon," Damon warns, gripping my flesh. "We don't know who's in there."

I slam on the brakes, and Silas nearly rear-ends us. I see him throw his hands up into the air in the rearview mirror.

"If you intend to hide me away like this every single time we encounter anything dangerous, then I'm not sure I want to be a part of this dynamic," I tell him honestly. The emotion in my voice is evident, and I blink back the tears as one of the cars behind Silas lays on the horn. "I can't just let a third of my heart walk into that house and be okay with it. I'm not a woman who needs protecting, Damon. I am a part of this team. I am scared as fuck about Jude, and I *need* to be there," I plead. I feel a tear run down my cheek. "I wasn't given that option growing up. Please don't hide me away. Let me help."

Damon's face is pinched with worry, but he nods once, and I sigh with relief. Taking my foot off the brake, I move us forward down the road to our house.

"If anything happens to any of you," Damon starts. He sighs, rubbing his mouth. "Whoever did this is going to pay."

"I know," I whisper. "They better be ready for our wrath. Welcome to the dark side of Savage Ink, motherfuckers."

I mean it as a joke, and when I look over at Damon briefly, his eyes are shining with pride, and *Damon Brooks is crying right now.* He sniffs, rubbing his face once with his hand before taking my free hand and squeezing it.

My heart aches, but I feel ready. I am tired of worrying.

We park at the curb one block away, just in case they're waiting for us. I see Silas pull behind us, and a third car–presumably Liam's–pull up behind him. We all get out and walk up the road to the house. I look behind me, scowling at Liam.

"I really wish he wasn't here," I growl to Silas, my voice low enough that I don't think Liam can hear.

"He's just as curious as we are," Silas responds. "I've known him most of my life, Lennon. He's a fucking shithead ninety-nine percent of the time, but I don't think he's lying about this."

Goosebumps drag along my skin, up to my neck. My skin tingles with anticipation, and I feel my heart begin to race again as we walk up the cement driveway. If Liam isn't involved... then who is?

"Stay behind us," Damon growls. I open my mouth to retort, but he clamps a rough hand over my mouth. "I mean it, princess. Now's not the time for arguing."

I nod, and he releases me. Silas unlocks the door silently, and we push it open.

Nothing.

There's no one waiting for us in the foyer, at least.

"Down to the chapel," Silas whispers, and the four of us walk quietly to the stone staircase leading to the Huxley chapel.

Silas goes down first, followed by Liam, and then Damon, who looks back at me every few seconds. I try not to roll my eyes. Once we get down into the chapel, my stomach sinks and roils.

The first thing I see is all the blood on the floor. I cup my mouth with my hand, holding back a sob.

Jude is here.

And he's nailed to the cross.

twenty-eight

Jude

"Jude."

I can't tell if her beautiful, pained voice is an apparition, or if it's real. I don't have the energy to open my eyes, and the full-body shivers have now subsided, giving way to a dull ache where he hammered my hands and feet to the wooden cross. It doesn't even hurt anymore–not if I don't move. My skin is attempting to heal, so every time I do move, it opens the wounds anew, sending a searing pain through my limbs. So, I stay still. Heavy. Exhausted. Numb.

"Jude." *Yes*, she's real.

I make a sound in the back of my throat to show that I'm alive, and I hear her rush over to me.

"Oh my God," she sobs, running a delicate hand over my skin. I'm sure she's trying to figure out how to get me out of this predicament. I almost laugh. *Good luck with that, princess. He hammered them in nicely.*

"I'm going to kill whoever did this to you." *Silas.*

"Jude?" Damon's hand comes up to my cheek, and I make another noise. "Who the *fuck* did this to you?"

"What the fuck," someone else says, and I slowly open my eyes. Liam fucking James.

"Was it him?" Lennon asks quickly, pointing at Liam. It takes everything in me to shake my head once. I see her body deflate a bit. I know she was hoping to blame him. Truth be told, it would be easier if it were him.

I make another noise with my mouth, my throat dry from screaming. Lennon grabs a bottle of water from her backpack and holds it up to me. I take a few small sips, the cool liquid coating my burning throat.

"Call the police," Liam says to Silas. "We need to figure out who did this."

"No," I rasp, wincing as the small movement of shaking my head pulls at the nails in my hand.

"Jude," Damon growls, looking me up and down. "Who." It's a command, not a question.

I look behind them, my eyes narrowing on the dark figure watching this all unfold from the back of the chapel. Lennon follows my gaze first, and then the three others twist around quickly.

"Hello, Silas," he taunts, and I hiss as my feet instinctually pull against the nails.

"Run," I mumble, warning them.

Liam looks back at me briefly before a bullet goes through his right arm.

twenty-nine

Lennon

I scream as the gunshot sounds, and Liam drops to the ground on my left. Damon and Silas grab me, pulling me down onto the floor and covering me with their bodies. I cover my ears and squeeze my eyes shut as someone walks up to us from the back of the chapel. Liam is sputtering and cursing next to me, but quite honestly, I'm more worried about Jude being hung up on a fucking cross, and the gun in the hands of the man behind us.

"You can get up. I won't kill you."

Silas and Damon climb off me tentatively, pulling me up and positioning themselves in front of me. Between them, I see a tall, middle-aged man in sweatpants and a hoodie. Silas stiffens in front of me, reaching back for my hand and squeezing it tightly.

"Samuel," Jude grits out.

Damon growls, and Silas doesn't let go of my hand.

"Hello, Samuel," Silas says slowly. His voice is cool and collected.

I glance down at Liam, who is gripping his arm and looking up at Samuel with what I assume is real terror.

Samuel fucking Kent.

He never disappeared–he's been here ever since.

My heart gallops against my ribs. My palms turn sweaty, and I wipe them on my pants. My eyes flick between Samuel–who is watching Silas with reverence–and Silas, who looks about three seconds away from wringing Samuel's neck.

As of 2003, no one has seen or heard from Samuel Kent.

I think back to the article. Samuel was Liam's predecessor. According to Damon and Silas, he was the original leader of the Church of the Rapture. Goosebumps prickle on my skin as I take in his appearance. Thin, tall, with silver scruff and light eyes. His hair is dark and peppered with white.

"What are you doing here, Samuel?" Silas's tone is not one of kind curiosity.

Samuel cocks his head and crosses his arms, the gun still in his right hand. "I don't think that's any way to treat an old family friend."

"Why are you here? Why Jude?"

Samuel shrugs, smirking. "I thought it would get your attention."

"That's why you've been posting on Instagram," I whisper. "This was a trap. You knew we'd come for Jude, so you led us to the cave so that you could do *this* to him." I curl and uncurl my fists as the puzzle pieces begin to form in my mind. I was here earlier tonight, and I didn't even look around, so focused on getting to the cave. Could I have saved Jude from this then? I feel the blood drain from my face as he nods, uncrossing his hands and playing with the trigger on the gun.

"Smart girl," he says softly. *Too* softly. "Those zealots wouldn't know their way around social media." He laughs. "But you. I underestimated you. And here I was, thinking they hired you to work the front desk because of your pretty face."

The air leaves my lungs. "You've been–you've been watching us."

Samuel chuckles, and Damon's hand finds mine in the dark, gripping it tightly. "I have. It's been highly entertaining. And shall I say... scandalous?" He wiggles his brows at me, and I feel like I'm going to vomit. I don't even have a chance to respond before he continues. "You were here earlier," he muses. "Had you showed up five minutes earlier, you would've heard Jude's screams before he passed out from the pain."

I'm going to be sick. Jude was here, and I just left him.

"Give us one reason why we shouldn't kill your fucking ass," Damon growls.

Silas grunts in agreement, but Samuel doesn't seem perturbed by his threat at all.

And that worries me.

Silas and Damon share a look, and I feel them push me back a couple of steps, telling me to retreat. I pretend like I'm checking on Jude, and when I look up at him briefly, he's watching me with sad eyes.

Samuel didn't just nail Jude's hands and feet to the cross.

He broke his soul.

I stroke Jude's face. "We'll get you help," I say softly

SAVAGE GODS

enough that the others can't hear me. "As soon as we take care of him."

Jude just squeezes his eyes shut and grits his teeth as a fresh wave of blood drips down his arm. It's two against one–three, if you count me. We need to get the gun from Samuel and call the cops. Looking at Damon, his eyes find mine. I nod once, and Damon looks back at Jude, anguish peppering his features. I see it then–Damon's wrath. He looks at Silas. Just as I'm about to cause a scene so that they can attack, they both rush forward, tackling Samuel in half a second, and my body goes rigid with worry.

I cover my head when I hear the gun go off again, terrified to open my eyes and see either of them hurt, but when I look up, Silas bends down and grabs the gun while Damon pins him to the floor. I hold my breath as I visually check all three of them for a bullet wound, but they're fine. *Thank fucking God.* Even Liam is watching from the fetal position, his face pained as he witnesses this all unfold.

"Alright, alright, you've proved your point," Samuel says with amusement. Damon smashes his face against the stone floor.

"And what point is that?" Silas asks, smirking. "That you're a sad sack of skin and bones? That karma always gets the bad guys?"

Samuel huffs. "Who says I'm the bad guy?"

Fury blasts through me, and I answer without thinking. "I'm pretty sure molesting a little boy makes you a bad guy," I hiss, glaring at Samuel. I can't imagine what Silas had to go through at such a young age–what *this* man did to him. It makes my chest feel like it's going to crack open. "Oh, and can't forget about *crucifying* Jude."

Samuel's eyes flick to mine, and he studies me for a

second before baring his teeth. "Did I ask for your opinion?" he seethes, and Silas presses the gun into the back of Samuel's neck.

"Let's get this over with," Silas commands, and I see Damon nod once.

They're going to kill him.

"Don't you want to know who ordered your parents to kill Oliver?" Samuel asks. Even though his face is being pressed into the stone floor, he sounds smug.

"It was you," Liam seethes.

"Hold on," Damon growls, shoving a knee into Samuel's back. "Are you saying this shithead is innocent?" He gestures to Liam.

Samuel looks at me and gives me an evil smile. *God, he's fucking creepy.*

"I never ordered anyone to kill anybody," Liam bites out. He's panting now, and I know we should probably get him an ambulance before he bleeds out. "You were so intent on hating me after–" He grinds his jaw together. "I'm not the monster here."

"I'm not discussing this right now," Silas retorts, glaring at Liam. "I still have issues with you and the church. This doesn't exonerate you." He turns to Samuel. "It was you."

Samuel wheezes and coughs, and I see blood trickle out of his mouth and onto the floor. He nods. "Your parents and I always remained close. They were the only people I trusted. Oliver was a mistake," he growls, looking at Liam. "I never would've held him in such high regard like this jackass. He needed to go. And your parents were more than happy to do it."

"You fucking asshole," Liam says, his voice frayed.

"The church is a disgrace because of you," Samuel spits in Liam's direction.

"Did you know?" Silas asks, pointing the gun at Liam. "Did you know my parents were in contact with Samuel, and that he ordered them to kill Oliver?"

Liam shakes his head. "No. But I had my suspicions, especially since your parents acted so out of character." He grimaces as he tries to sit up. "They betrayed me. The three of them played all of us."

"Your day is coming," Samuel responds, clear as day. "You're all sinners. Every person in this room. I tried to help Jude, tried to get him to walk away from the church and join me. The church today is full of transgressing bastards because of him. It's not the same church I started, and it hasn't been for a long time. But Jude refused," he adds, his voice soft as he looks over at where Jude is hanging, head drooped. My heart cracks in half at the sight. "He left me no choice but to prove a gruesome point."

I feel my palms tighten into fists as fiery rage simmers within me. Jude. Silas. Damon–the three men that I love. And he's already hurt two of them. I won't let him hurt anyone else.

"Oh, and you're so perfect?" I yell, walking up to him. "If God is real, and Heaven is real, you're going to Hell. No true God would want you to ascend to Heaven, you piece of shit."

Samuel's light gray eyes find mine. "You're a little bitch, aren't you?" I stiffen. "You're the worst of them all, laying with men before marriage. We had a word for you in the olden days. *Whore*. That's all you'll ever be good at."

Silas pulls the trigger before he can say another word, and I see the stain of blood seeping through Samuel's shoulder before I realize what happened.

"Fuck!" Samuel screams, writhing in pain.

"I wasn't sure I was going to kill you, but then you went and called our partner a whore, so I think I speak for all of us when I say, I hope this fucking hurts. Go to hell, Samuel."

Silas shoots him in the other shoulder, his aim near perfect. I look up at him with wide eyes, and he just winks at me before shooting him a third time in the thigh.

Samuel screams, curling into a ball, and Damon stands up and runs over to Jude. I see him pull his phone out to call an ambulance.

Silas drops the gun and rushes over to me, pulling me in for a hug. "He'll bleed out in a couple of minutes," he murmurs into my ear, his hand cupping my head against him.

I smile. "That's the sexiest thing you've ever said."

We both rush over to Jude. There's not much we can do until the paramedics get here, and when I look back at Samuel a minute later, he's dead—a pool of blood surrounding him.

"This was self-defense," Damon growls, pointing at Liam. "Understood?"

Liam nods. His face is completely white, and he looks at Silas like he's seeing him for the first time. Silas glares at him but doesn't say anything.

Four paramedics rush down the stairs, and they all stop when they see Jude on the cross.

"Fuck me," one of them mutters.

Damon explains the situation, and Silas pulls me into the corner with an arm around my shoulder. They manage to cut away the nails as delicately as possible, bandaging Jude's hands and feet in gauze before placing him on a board to carry him to the ambulance. One of them covers

Samuel with a sheet, and the other gets Liam sorted on his own board.

"I should go with Jude," I whisper, pulling away from Silas.

He tugs me back, kissing me on the brow. "We all go. We're all in this together."

thirty

Lennon

It takes Jude a few hours to come to, after multiple rounds of IV fluids and blood transfusions. He lost quite a bit of blood, and his left hand is fractured from the nail, but the doctor tells us that he'll be fine after a tetanus booster. The police also stop by to get statements from each of us. We tell them the truth–Samuel did this to Jude, we found him in the basement, and we were able to get the gun from him after he shot Liam. Silas is the one that elaborates on what happens next, saying Samuel threatened me and he had no choice but to shoot him. Luckily, Samuel has been in trouble with the law for some time, so no one asks too many questions.

By the time they leave us alone in Jude's recovery room, I'm exhausted and falling asleep on Damon's shoulder. Silas spoke to the head nurse, and I'm pretty sure they all have crushes on the guys because they don't ask us to leave, even though visiting hours were over a long time ago.

"Hey," Jude whispers, his voice ragged.

I sit up and place a hand on his forehead. "Hi."

"I'm not going to be able to use my hand for a while, huh?" he asks, and I can hear the devastation in his voice. I hate to say it, but the studio never even crossed my mind during all of this. For Jude, though, creating art is his life.

"A few weeks," Silas answers, standing up and leaning against Jude's bed.

"Fucking Samuel Kent," Jude huffs, looking away. His eyes are watery, and he sniffs twice before looking down.

"But you're alive," I say quietly, running my fingers gently through his hair.

He nods. "I know." He gives me a tight smile. "We should let my clients know."

I nod. "I'll take care of everything later. I promise."

The task of calling up every single client scheduled for the next six to eight weeks seems daunting, but I'm more than willing to do it for him.

"Gave us quite a scare," Damon adds, sitting on the foot of Jude's bed, being sure not to touch his injured feet.

Jude shakes his head and sighs. "It was crazy. One minute, I was walking to my car from the meeting–"

"Where were you?" I ask, interrupting him.

"Boston." His eyes find mine, and he nods when my mouth falls open. "Yeah. They have a whole following there, so they opened a church recently in the old part of town." I shake my head. *Of course they did.* "Anyway, Samuel walked up to me in the parking garage, clocked me with a gun, and the next thing I knew, he was dragging me down the stairs to the chapel."

"How the fuck did he get inside?" Silas asks, his hand rubbing his mouth.

"My keys."

"We need to change the locks," Damon growls, punching in a text to someone.

"I wasn't expecting him. I left Liam and the other leaders in their office, so I had my guard down." He pauses, wincing. "The first hand hurt, and I almost got away, but he's fucking strong. He held me down, and by the time both hands were in, I sort of gave up," he admits sheepishly. "Anyway, he just sat in the back of the chapel, silent and still. I knew he was waiting for you. I was in and out of consciousness, but then I heard your voice..." He looks over at me, his gaze filled with awe that warms my chest. "I thought I was dreaming."

"Fucking hell," Silas says, pushing off the bed and pacing around the small hospital room. "This whole time I thought it was Liam."

"Liam's not innocent, either," Jude adds, his voice low and guttural. "During the meeting, there was talk of the darker side of the church. Just like we suspected."

"He told you all of that?" Damon asks incredulously.

Jude huffs a laugh. "No way. You know me, I'd been planning this for months. I slipped a small microphone into Liam's shirt pocket when he picked me up this morning. I was listening to the recordings as I walked to my car, so I didn't get to hear everything, but it's not great. I mean, yes, it doesn't seem like he was the one who ordered your parents to murder Oliver, but he's not innocent."

Silas stops and rubs his face. "We need to get some sleep." He glances at me pointedly. "All of us."

I shake my head. "I want to stay." I see the resignation on his face as he nods. "I would stay for any of you," I add, my voice breaking. Then I feel a tear trail down my cheek, and Jude reaches a bandaged hand up to my arm.

"Don't cry for me, princess. I promise I'll be able to use this hand on you soon."

I burst out laughing. "There's the Jude I know and love."

The air in the room intensifies then, and I look between Silas and Damon. "I love him—and I love you both." I release a long, slow breath. "There. I said it."

Damon is the first one to move, and he pulls me into a tight hug. "We love you, Lennon."

"Lennon fucking Rose," is all Silas says.

I feel him come up behind me and wrap his arms around my waist. I close my eyes, breathing in their scents and their comforting mass of muscle.

"I'd hug you too, but..." Jude trails off, and our laughs echo off the small hospital walls.

———

A few hours later, after Silas and Damon go home, I wake up to Jude singing *Hey Jude* by the Beatles.

"Really?" I ask, smiling as I walk over to his bed as he sings. I swallow as my throat constricts with emotion for how strongly I feel for him. Taking his hand, I gently pull it to my lips and kiss it. "I was so worried," I whisper, my voice breaking on the last word. "I thought the worst all day long. I was convinced Liam had murdered you and left your body to rot somewhere." I can't hold in the sob that leaves me, which quickly turns into a laugh.

"Nah, I could've taken Liam. Samuel, though... he surprised me."

I open and close my mouth, trying to decide how to ask the question I'm about to ask. "Does this mean you're done going undercover for Church of the Rapture?"

Jude looks down at his blanket. "Not until we take them all down. Remember, Liam broke into your apartment, Lennon. He *threatened* you. He may seem tame compared to Samuel, but that's only because Samuel was a sociopath. Liam is still a threat to us."

I grind my jaw. As much as I hate the idea of Jude going back into the fire, at least I know Liam probably won't kidnap him after what happened.

"Come here," he says softly, scooting his body to one side of the bed.

"I don't want to hurt you." I look down at his bandaged hands, trying not to laugh when I realize he reminds me of Edward Scissorhands.

"Get in here, princess." His voice is so tender in this moment, and he looks up at me with wide, pleading eyes. He needs this more than I do. Being mindful of his injuries, I snuggle up against his warm body. He wraps his arms around me slowly. "The whole time I was in the chapel, I was going in and out of consciousness. I just kept thinking... what if I never see Lennon again?"

"Jude–" He stops me with a quick, but no less treasuring kiss.

"Don't get me wrong. It made me sad about Silas and Damon too. They're like brothers to me–they're my partners in life. You all are. But something about you..." he trails off, kissing the top of my head. I squeeze my eyes shut, my chest aching when I think about what the outcome could've been. "It made me realize that I want you, Lennon. All of you. I'm so fucking in love with you. I want to get married and have babies with you–"

I open my mouth to respond to his declaration, my eyes watering again, but he continues.

"I know. You can't marry three different men. You know

what I mean. Some sort of civil ceremony. No laws, just a celebration of our commitment to each other. You, me, Silas, and Damon."

I'm too stunned to speak. Jude sighs.

"Maybe it's silly. Just ignore me–" He shakes his head slightly, but I can tell he's serious.

"Are you asking me to marry you?" I whisper, looking up at him, my mouth agape.

Jude laughs. "Yes, except it wouldn't be a legal marriage, I guess–"

I sit up and take his face in my hands, kissing him slowly and with meaning, my tongue swirling into his mouth as he moans. I pull away and grin.

"I love that idea. Maybe we can ask the guys what they think?"

Jude smirks. "They already know. We talked about it before you even moved in."

My heart stumbles a bit. "You did?"

"Much to our chagrin, Lennon Rose, we ended up really liking you from day one. Loving you, even."

My chest rises and falls as I look down into his eyes. "Let's do it, then."

thirty-one

Lennon

"What the hell happened?" Briar storms into the house, Easton on her hip. Jude is sitting in the formal living room, and I suppose Silas must've told Ledger what transpired, because the four of them come marching in after her. "When did you get out of the hospital?" she demands, looking between all of us.

"Three days ago," I explain.

Ledger looks between Silas and me. "So it was Samuel." His tone is curt, and I know he isn't directing it at me. I'm sure it's a shock to him, just like it was for Silas. "And you killed him?"

"I did," Silas answers from his place in the door of the kitchen.

Ledger sighs, walking over to him and pulling him into a tight bear hug. "Good fucking riddance, brother."

We all sit around and have lunch as Silas tells his

version of the story. When we get to the part about the paramedics taking Jude away, Briar leans in and whispers into my ear.

"So, does that mean the altar is gone?" I cover my mouth before I laugh out loud, nodding once. She groans and continues to breastfeed Easton next to me.

We've already told Lola the abridged version of the events, and she's helping me reach out to their clients. True to form, Silas and Damon only took one night off after everything happened, so they're back at Savage Ink every single night while I tend to Jude. Lola has taken over some of my shifts. She's also taught them how to use the damn scheduler, so they're not floundering there by themselves.

I've briefly updated Mindy, too, though she got the light, PG version. I'll tell her everything one day, but with Liam still out there, and Jude still undercover… I have to be careful who knows what, and how much.

I hold Easton while Briar goes to the restroom, and Damon sidles up to me as Ledger and Silas chat. Jude is asleep in his chair—the pain meds are no joke. Samson, Ash, and Hunter are in the kitchen cleaning up the lunch dishes.

"I swear, this kid gets cuter and cuter every time I see him."

"I know," I coo, bouncing the smiling baby on my knee. He giggles, and I can't help but hug him tightly. "I want to eat you up," I squeal, pretending to bite his thighs, which then makes him laugh even louder.

"You're going to make one hell of a mom one day, Lennon."

Damon's words rush through me, causing my heart rate to go wild. "Oh?"

He smirks, taking Easton from me. "Yeah. Might be fun to have a kid with you." I don't know what to say to that. Instead of answering, I play with the fringe on my cutoff shorts. "I know it's scary," he murmurs. "Our parents were such dickheads." I swallow thickly and nod. Damon has never really spoken about his parents, and neither has Jude. Whenever I've asked, they've just said they both had normal Greythorn upbringings, and sadly, I know exactly what they mean. "Your mom…" He blows out a loud breath of air. "You'll be nothing like her. None of us will because we know what not to do. We can break the cycle. It ends with you–with *us*."

He nuzzles Easton's nose, which causes Easton to grab it and pull. Damon feigns a soft yell, which makes Easton giggle again. My heart swells.

I never thought of it that way—of breaking the cycle. But he's right. For so long, I was worried about turning into my mother. And when I thought about parenthood, I thought about my childhood, which wasn't good. But we could be great parents for our own child, because, like Damon said, we know what not to do.

An hour later, we say goodbye to Briar and the guys. They all climb into a big SUV, and I smile as the five of them fuss over Easton and his car seat. Closing the door, I turn around to find Jude watching me from his place in the living room.

"Good morning, sunshine," I joke.

He smiles and stretches, wincing as his hands accidentally brush together briefly. Walking over to him, I take a seat next to him on the couch. Silas and Damon are talking in the kitchen, so I lean over and kiss him. His wrist comes to my neck, pulling me closer.

"We should be careful," I warn, pulling away.

He growls in response. "I don't want to be fucking careful, Lennon. I want to fuck you senseless."

His words send a shockwave of electricity through me. "Jude, we should make sure your hands and feet are—"

"Get on your knees, then." His eyes search mine, and gone is the humor, the jokes, the sweetness. Right now, he's just a man with a primal need to feel something. To feel *me*.

"Okay." I climb down from the couch and get on my knees between his legs, my thighs clenching.

"Well, well, well," Damon says from behind me. I twist around, and he gives me a lopsided smile. He walks over to where I'm kneeling in front of Jude. "Keep going. Don't stop on my account."

I smile, bending down to pull Jude's sweatpants off. I've been helping him shower, but we haven't crossed this line yet. I didn't want to hurt him. Right now, though? He's watching me like a savage predator. His eyes are narrow and grow dark as I pull his hard cock out.

"Suck it," Damon commands from behind me.

Looking up at him, I notice Silas watching from the far side of the room, a smirk on his face as he dries a wine glass.

I bend down and take Jude into my mouth fully, letting out a small moan, reveling in the feel of his piercings on my tongue as he moves his hips, sheathing himself deep in my throat.

"I fucking love when you moan for me, princess," he growls.

Damon wraps his arms around my middle, kneeling behind me as his calloused fingers trace circles on my skin.

I hear Silas come to my right side, and I pop Jude out of

my mouth, pulling my shirt and bra off quickly. I stand, stepping out of my shorts and underwear, and then kneel back down in front of Jude. His mouth is half open, a lopsided smile making him look unnervingly handsome.

Damon's hand caresses my ass as I bend forward, pulling Jude back into my mouth. This time, he hisses, a tight moan escaping his lips.

"Shit," he rasps unevenly. "This feels so fucking good." I can smell the coconut body wash that I used, and I feel emotional as I look up at him, his cock in my mouth. He grins, fisting my hair. "Good girl."

I missed this.

Damon and Silas get behind me, and I release Jude again while we figure out the positioning.

"One second," Silas says, running up the stairs.

Damon gets naked, lying down with his head near Jude's feet. "Ride me," he commands, and I straddle him. Scooting lower, I grab his massive cock and tease my entrance for a second. "I wouldn't do that if I were you," he growls, grabbing my hand and holding it at my side. Thrusting quickly, he fills me to the hilt, and I cry out.

I feel Silas behind me, hearing his belt buckle first. Damon moves out of me, and I look up at Jude, my eyes fluttering closed, as Damon drives into me again.

Silas comes behind me, pushing me forward so that I'm on my hands, which just so happens to be the perfect height to take Jude's glorious cock back into my mouth.

"You're so beautiful," Silas mutters, running a hand over my bare ass. I arch my back and eagerly wrap my lips around Jude's length just as Silas slowly enters my ass. So agonizingly slowly, the sensation making me gasp.

Damon relaxes his pace too, as I get used to the double penetration, and his hands come up to my nipples. Silas continues to stretch me, and soon the stinging gives way to an out-of-body feeling of pleasure. I'm so full of them—ass, pussy, and mouth—and I wouldn't have it any other way.

"Fuck," Damon cries, his thumbs grazing my nipples. "I can feel your pussy milking me, princess."

"Do you like it when we're both inside of you?" Silas murmurs, brushing my hair off my back, and I nod lazily, whimpering. The feeling is so dizzying, with Silas and Damon both inside of me, feeling the way Jude's piercings massage the back of my throat when I take him in deeply, and the subsequent noises he makes...

I moan, letting Silas and Damon move in and out of me rhythmically. "I love it," I finally answer as run my tongue down Jude's swollen shaft.

"Holy fuck," Jude groans, his voice frayed as I take him into my mouth again, sucking hard. "Watching this is going to make me come."

I pull off his cock, using a hand instead so I can watch him come all over himself. I use my spit as lube, and my eyes flutter closed as Damon ups his tempo from underneath me. Silas squeezes my ass, pulling me onto his cock. It's so intense—and when I work my hand faster, using my other hand for support, Jude's mouth falls open, and he begins to fuck my hand. Damon is moaning with every thrust, and I can tell by his stiffening shaft that he's about to come, too. Silas is roughly using me to fuck his cock, and I'm being pulled in three different directions as Jude's cock twitches in my grasp.

It turns to steel as it pulses, streams of come shooting a foot into the air as his head falls back and he cries out. I continue to work my hand, slowing down, making sure to get the head of his length with every movement, and it makes him twitch. Watching him come undone like this, seeing him alive and healing, makes my orgasm begin to crest inside of me. My toes curl at my sides, and I use some of Jude's come to work my clit as the world tilts a bit. My pussy squeezes Damon's cock as he comes, slamming into me and making me scream.

Damon growls as I soak his chest, a stream of liquid shooting out of me as I convulse on top of him.

"Fuck," Silas says roughly. "I can feel it in your ass." Then I feel him coming, too. He pulls me onto his cock, his hips hitting my ass, he's so deep, and I can feel both him and Damon filling me with their come.

"That's it, princess," Silas says into my ear, kissing my neck and slapping my ass.

"That was really fucking hot," Jude muses, his head still lying against the couch.

"Fuck," Damon growls, slipping out of me.

Silas pulls out, too, and I stand up. Damon helps to clean me, which is hard because my legs are still shaking. It's a sight to behold—seeing Silas clean Jude up and watching as Damon cleans me up. We really are a team.

These men—these godly, strong, alpha men—are mine. All three of them. Even though we almost lost Jude, I never want to forget this moment.

We help Jude upstairs to Silas's bed, which happens to be a king. Somehow, we all manage to squeeze onto it without hurting Jude. Even though it's only three in the afternoon, I know we all need a nap. Today, and this whole week in general, has been exhausting. I find myself sleeping more and napping daily, which is never something I used to do. I know Silas and Damon will be headed to Savage at six-thirty, but for now, we're all here.

I wrap my arms around Jude, and Silas wraps his arms around me. I feel Damon wrap his arms around Silas.

This.

I could stay like this forever.

Closing my eyes, I smile as we all fall asleep together.

They are my past colliding with my present—and hopefully my future.

thirty-two

Liam

I grimace as I grab a glass from the cupboard in my kitchen using my left arm—my only good arm. Panting, I fill it with water, gulping every drop. After I set the glass down, I close my eyes and take a few deep breaths, but even that fucking hurts.

"He himself bore our sins in his body on the cross, so that we might die to sins and live for righteousness; by his wounds you have been healed," I mutter to myself. Pushing off the counter, I slowly make my way upstairs to my bedroom. Just lifting the duvet has me hissing in pain thanks to the bullet wound in my right arm. It lodged itself deep into my bicep, sitting nicely in the folds of muscle. Even tiny, miniscule movements with the right side of my body cause it to ache and throb.

I also lost a lot of blood, refusing the blood transfusion because of my religious exemption, which only adds to my pain and weakness. I slowly get into bed, being mindful of my bad arm. Lying on my left side, I take another deep breath, reciting the same line in my head over and over. *So Christ, having been offered once to bear the sins of many, will appear a second time, not to deal with sin but to save those who are eagerly waiting for him.*

And when he comes for me, I will be ready. I can't stand the thought of having unholy blood running through my body—the blood of *sinners*.

My phone rings on my nightstand, and I open my eyes to see Yuri's name flash on the screen. Yuri—a man of his word. A *Godly* man. A friend. And maybe in another life… a lover.

I slide my finger across the screen to answer.

"Any news?"

Yuri grumbles on the other end of the line. "Yes. I found something you should know about."

I slowly sit up in bed. "Oh?"

"I was able to ascertain the serial number, thanks to a friend. It seems the microphone was purchased online."

I snort. "That's all he was able to ascertain? I thought you said he was good—"

"It was purchased online using a credit card in Jude Vanderbilt's name." I swallow once. Twice. My cheeks heat with humiliation. "Liam? Did you hear me?"

"That lying rat bastard," I growl.

"How shall we proceed?" Yuri asks.

I sigh, rubbing my lips with my good hand. "We do nothing for now. We feel him out, push him, see how long it is before he cracks."

"Liam, with all due respect, I don't think we can crack this kid."

He's probably right. After all, it appears even I was duped. The hesitation, the worry about the afterlife, the things he confessed to me… it was all a lie. A very good one at that. Even Silas, Damon, and Lennon put on a good show for me. Grinding my jaw, I hang my head. I was an idiot to trust him. To trust them.

Silas's words from that night run through my mind.

I still have issues with you and the church. This doesn't exonerate you.

He knew. Jude knew. The texts from Jude over the last couple of days, asking me how I was feeling… it was part of the ruse.

"Then we get better than him and play him at his own game. And we silence them—*all* of them—once and for all."

Yuri mumbles his agreement before hanging up, and I set my phone down on the duvet as I stare at the wall in front of me.

Samuel played me, made me believe he'd run away, that he remained in hiding. He took my good friends and turned them against the church. He coerced them into murdering an innocent man. As much as I didn't agree with what Oliver was doing, murder never once became a possibility in my mind. I never would've suspected the Huxley's were guilty, that they would betray me like that. I did my part to ensure they stayed out of jail, but after that, they were dead to me. The fury of being lied to by my friends—the embarrassment…

And now Jude? Silas?

I never wanted to find out the hard way. To find out the truth after the fact.

I refuse to stay in the dark and be played like that.

Again.

They're probably all laughing about it together, too, in their fucked up, sinful little relationship. Before, I took issue with Silas. But now? They're all a problem for me.

They think they can spy on me with a microphone? That I wouldn't find it in the hospital, sitting on the table, because one of the paramedics thought to save it when they cut my shirt off in the ambulance? I'm sure Jude thinks he won. Except he made one tiny mistake.

He got caught by Samuel. Tortured. *Crucified*. He wasn't thinking clearly, otherwise I'm sure he would've ensured I never found it. He would've ensured I never knew of his betrayal.

But he underestimated me.

I am a powerful man.

I have powerful connections—connections that would make Samuel Kent shake in his boots. I never needed to use them until now.

If they thought Samuel was bad, they have no idea what I'm capable of.

I must rid the world of these sinners.

I kneel before my bed, bringing my hands together and breathing through the pain.

"There is no faithfulness, no love, no acknowledgment of God. There is only cursing, lying and murder, stealing and adultery. They break all bounds, and bloodshed follows bloodshed."

TO BE CONTINUED...

Thank you so much for reading! I hope you enjoyed the second book in the Savage Hearts series, and seeing Lennon's relationship with her three Gods develop even further. There's a lot more of their relationship coming in

Savage Reign. I've had the epilogue scene in my mind since before I started the series, and I cannot *wait* for you to read it. ;)

You can download Savage Reign, book three of the Savage Hearts series, below:

Savage Reign

Also, don't forget to sign up for my mailing list! There are monthly giveaways, exclusive excerpts, and I share news there before anywhere else! It's the best place to keep in touch with me.

Mailing List

Thank you so much for reading!!

Have you read my Ruthless Royals duet? Did you know it's also set in Greythorn, MA? If you want to see how everything unfolded with Briar, Hunter, Ledger (Silas' brother), Ash, and Samson, keep reading for an excerpt from book one!

Blurb:

Their names are whispers in the hallways.
Hunter, Ash, Ledger, and Samson.
The *Kings*.

Four of the most beautiful men I've ever seen, with cruel agendas and an even crueler reign over Ravenwood Academy.
Wreaking havoc in our small, New England town, no one asks questions.
For the most part, people ignore or avoid them.
After all, they're royalty here.
Because one of them—the cruelest one—is the headmaster's son.
And my new stepbrother.
They can try to torment me.
They can try to break me.
But they have no idea what I've endured.
They're used to getting whatever their ruthless, little hearts desire.
Maybe I should keep my mouth shut.
Maybe I should let them win.
But I'm not afraid of getting my hands dirty.
Lord knows I'm used to it by now.
My name is Briar Monroe, and these Kings are about to find out just how fucked up this Queen can be.

Ruthless Crown is full-length high-school bully reverse harem romance. It is book one of the Ruthless Royals duet, and while it doesn't end with a true cliffhanger, there are unanswered questions. It is advised to read them in order. Please note Ruthless Crown contains explicit language, bullying, and flashbacks of abuse/trauma. It also features four hot AF guys who would do anything to protect their feisty Queen. The duet will have a HEA.

Download the Ruthless Royals Duet

Briar

"Shit," Jack whispers, glancing at the row of lockers in front of us. "We have company."

I look up and notice Hunter leaning against a locker, glaring at me. *How did he know I'd be here?*

Something fiery shoots through me at that gaze, and I notice Ash, Ledger, and Samson standing near the other wall of lockers.

"Let me guess," I murmur to Jack. "That's my locker?"

"I told you," Scarlett hisses. "They're not going to leave you alone."

I grind my teeth together and clench my fists. "This is ridiculous," I whisper. "I'm putting my foot down."

I stalk over to where Hunter is standing, arms crossed. "Excuse me," I order, not breaking eye contact. There's nothing kind in his expression, and his jaw ticks ever so slightly. A few people stop to watch us, their expressions stunned.

"You're excused," he muses, his face dripping with disdain.

My pulse speeds up, and anger flares through me. "This is my locker."

He tilts his head, and his eyes flash with amusement for a split second. "Yeah. I thought that was obvious."

Looking over his shoulder, I notice his friends watching me haughtily. *Okay, so they truly think of themselves as the rulers here, then? They sure have the arrogance to match it.*

"What do you want, Hunter?" I sigh, crossing my arms.

He chuckles, and the sound is both terrifying and thrilling. He reaches into his back pocket, pulling out a few folded pieces of paper. Handing them to me, he gives me a savage smile before I look down and take them. Willing my hands not to shake, I open the paper. My heart thumps against my ribs, and a flush works its way up my neck.

Snapping my eyes up to him, I pin him beneath an angry gaze. "You went through my diary?"

My diary—detailing the inappropriate dream I had about him the other night.

He crosses his arms and shrugs. "If you wanted me so badly, why didn't you just ask?"

Oh, the nerve...

"You wish," I growl, getting ready to turn and walk away.

Just as I move, he grabs the hand with the papers and tugs me into his hard body. Leaning down, his breath fans against my forehead.

"Tell me, just how wet did you get for me in that dream of yours?" To my horror, he raises his other hand, and a pink, lacy thong—*my* thong—dangles from his fingers.

My mouth goes dry, and my heart wallops against my chest as I close my eyes.

No. No, no, no.

Grabbing my underwear, I twist away from him and turn to walk away. Tears prick at my eyes, but I take a deep breath. I refuse to give them the satisfaction of knowing they got to me. Scarlett and Jack usher me out of the hallway, but before I get to the door, I feel a presence behind me.

"I told him not to do it."

I turn. One of the Kings—the one with the glasses—walks up to me. *Samson Hall.*

"He's lashing out. Give it a few days."

"You can tell him I won't tolerate this shit for a few more days."

"He won't listen."

I clench my teeth. "Why? Just leave me alone."

Samson laughs and shakes his head. "The more you resist, the more interesting you are to him, little lamb."

Hey little lamb, come out and play.

And then he turns around and walks back toward where Hunter is still watching me, and the four of them head off in the other direction.

Was he talking about Hunter, or himself? I certainly don't trust any of them.

I glare in their direction, and Scarlett and Jack tug me toward the entrance of the hallway. I'm still fuming as I shove my underwear into my backpack. When I finally look at Scarlett and Jack, my pulse has slowed and I take a deep, calming breath.

"This is war," I declare, ignoring the look Jack and Scarlett share.

I have a really sickening feeling that this is going to be a long year.

Keep reading here...

acknowledgments

Thank you to Renee and Ashleigh, who read the first version of this book! Your suggestions have been total lifesavers, especially that pesky last chapter.

Ashleigh, thank you for all of your help with keeping me organised and keeping my head on straight. I could not have done this without you.

Mackenzie, as always, thank you for the edits! I always love your suggestions, and I will forever be grateful for the way you were flexible for this book! It saved me from total and complete burnout.

Emma, thank you for the gorgeous cover!! *heart eyes*

Wander, your images bring these characters to life.

To my husband, who helped iron out the ending of this book and plot book 3. You're always willing to help me when I'm stuck, and I will forever be grateful that I married someone who fights for me, who encourages me to follow my dreams, and who reads every single word I write. I love you.

To Jasmine, I feel like you deserve a shout out for being one of my biggest supporters. Silas is yours. <3

To my family—my sister, dad, in-laws, and grandparents. Thank you for always believing in me. And my mom—this was a hard winter without you, but your last words to me are forever cemented in my mind. It's because of you that I am going to be a full-time writer this year. I love you, and I miss you every single minute of every single day.

To my readers, I love all of you so much.

And to my Dark Hearts, thank you for encouraging me to dive into reverse harem. It's been an amazing, wild ride!

Last but not lease, to my author friends. Thank you for sharing my books, for reading (it always blows my mind in the best way!) and all of the private messages and texts. You guys are the best, and you inspire me each and every day. I love it when this community comes together to lift each other up. *Virtual hugs about the author*

Amanda Richardson writes from her chaotic dining room table in Yorkshire, England, often distracted by her husband and two adorable sons. When she's not writing contemporary and dark, twisted romance, she enjoys coffee (a little too much) and collecting house plants like they're going out of style.

You can visit my website here: www.authoramandarichardson.com

Facebook: http://www.facebook.com/amandawritesbooks

For news and updates, please sign up for my newsletter here!

also by amanda richardson

Love at Work Series:

Between the Pages

A Love Like That

Tracing the Stars

Say You Hate Me

HEATHENS Series (Dark Romance):

SINNERS

HEATHENS

MONSTERS

VILLAINS (coming 2023)

Standalones:

The Realm of You

The Island

Dirty Doctor

Ruthless Royals Duet (Reverse Harem):

Ruthless Crown

Ruthless Queen

Savage Hearts Series (Reverse Harem)

Savage Hate

Savage Gods

Savage Reign

Shadow Pack Series (Paranormal Romance, under my pen name K. Easton):

Shadow Wolf

Shadow Bride

Shadow Queen

Printed in Great Britain
by Amazon